DARK SHADOWS

Ever since agent Daniel Myers had fled from Turkey with stolen secret papers vital for Western interests and entered Bulgaria, he had been aware of a certain disturbing atmosphere. Bulgaria was a place that was steeped in the old ways and ancient, dark gypsy beliefs and superstitions. A time-haunted land of mystery and evil in which the Western, modern way of life seemed to hold little sway. Things happened here. Inexplicably terrible things which were mentioned only in hushed whispers by frightened peasants.

With his pursuers hot on his heels, and almost certain death awaiting him if he was caught, Myers took refuge with an isolated gypsy community—only to face an even greater peril that would challenge his sanity…

WILDSIDE PRESS BOOKS BY EDMUND GLASBY

The Ash Murders
The Chaos of Chung-Fu
The Dyrysgol Horror and Other Weird Tales
Ghouls of the Undercity
Labyrinth of The Lost
The Weird Shadow Over Morecambe

DARK SHADOWS

Occult Mystery Stories

EDMUND GLASBY

WILDSIDE PRESS

For the Hannah boys.

Published by Wildside Press LLC.
www.wildsidebooks.com

CONTENTS

DARK SHADOWS

*There were things more dangerous
than the men who were after him.*

"*What the hell!?*" Daniel Myers screamed savagely and slammed his foot down hard on the brakes. Tyres screeching, the steering wheel became a living thing in his hands as the car went into a violent spin, the dark blur that had rushed out in front of his headlights leaping into the undergrowth. With a series of bone-jarring bumps, the vehicle careened completely off the road, hit a decline, threatened to upend completely and then crashed down onto all four wheels. Wiry bushes clawed at the windscreen and windows on either side before, with a resounding crunch and the shattering of glass, the car smashed into a tree.

The violent impact threw Myers forward. The seatbelt he was wearing snapped free from its mooring and he was propelled from his seat and flung hard against the windscreen, smashing straight through it as though he had been tugged from the vehicle by invisible ropes. Narrowly missing the tree, he flew, head first for several yards before splashing down into a muddy, weed-choked pool.

Had Myers been unconscious he would undoubtedly have drowned. Bubbling mud from his mouth and nostrils, he painfully raised his head and began gasping for air. Blood trickled from his gashed forehead and yet, miraculously, despite the severity of the crash, he was not that badly injured. Getting to his feet, he winced as he withdrew a nasty-looking shard of glass from his hand.

Suddenly remembering the shadowy thing that had sprung out into the road, he staggered back to the car. It had been little more than a pile of rust when he had stolen it from a side-street in Polski Trambesh, one of Bulgaria's larger towns, in order to hasten his getaway. Now it was just a crumpled wreck. Streams of black smoke billowed out from under the bonnet. With a fierce tug, he managed to get the driver's door open. Reaching inside, he opened the glove compartment and took out a small automatic, checked that it was fully loaded, then slipped it into his pocket. He then retrieved from the passenger seat the slim black leather case which contained the secret files.

More than a handful of good men had died for the sake of these documents and he was going to make damn sure that they had not died in vain. There had been terrible moments back in Istanbul when it had appeared that the entire mission was doomed to failure and only he had managed to escape. However, agents from the other side were closing in. Of this he had no doubt. Had he been more cautious in his dealing with the border guards at the Turkish-Bulgarian border he could well have been in Sofia right now, preparing to board a plane bound for London or Paris. Instead, he was embroiled in this fiendish game of cat-and-mouse, trying to pick his way slowly and steadily along the seldom-used back roads. And now look where his plans had got him.

The thought almost broke him in half but he knew it would do him no good to mull over past decisions. He had to get moving. Glancing at his watch, he saw that it was just after nine o'clock.

What that thing that had leapt out in front of him had been he had no idea although he was fairly certain that it had not been a human being. Although he had only seen it for a brief, flashing moment there had been something *disturbing* about its appearance and action. It was almost as if it had intentionally thrown itself into his path in order to cause him to veer off the road, indifferent to its own safety.

An unwelcome chill crept down his spine. Shaking a little, he looked around him, taking in his immediate surroundings, contemplating his next move. It was densely wooded. At the edge of the luminosity provided by the car headlights lay what appeared to be an expanse of marshland, the ground covered by a low lying mist. Dripping trees, covered with net-like growths of trailing weed and glistening, green algae grew on some of the tussocks of firmer ground. From all around could be heard plopping sounds as foul marsh gases belched and bubbled. There was a fetid reek in the air.

Cursing the fact that he was not in possession of a torch, Myers began to claw his way up the slope which had been carved by the car when it had come off the road. There was a jolting pain in his right leg and blood was trickling from his gashed forehead.

Upon reaching the road, he screwed up his eyes, scanning both directions. To his left and right the road disappeared in a black river of midnight, the tall trees that bordered it looming menacingly as though possessed of their own malign spirits. Here, the darkness seemed to lie more thickly, more tangibly, than anywhere else; as if it were a physical thing that pressed down upon him from all sides. He was glad of the automatic in his pocket and closed his fingers tightly around it as he stood there for a moment, deliberating whether to head back or venture on. Unfortunately, his geographical knowledge of this area was virtually non-existent. However, the last settlement he had passed through must have been at least thirty kilometres back and he had seen no other traffic on the road. Something which, initially, he had taken as a blessing but now he was not so sure.

Myers made up his mind quickly. He would set off in the other direction, in the hope that he would soon reach a village or town. If he was lucky, he might be able to flag down a passing motorist, in which case he would not be averse to using whatever violence was necessary in order to commandeer their vehicle.

It was a cloudy night and there was little moonlight and, as Myers set off, he could not dispel the feeling of horror that seeped into his mind. Whether it was due to that strange thing that he had seen earlier or whether it was down to the dark and the overall level of eeriness that seemed to pervade everything, he could not tell. He had to admit that ever since he had fled from Turkey and entered Bulgaria, he had been aware of a certain difference in the general atmosphere of the country. For this was a place that was steeped in the old ways and traditions. The ancient, dark gypsy beliefs and superstitions. To him it was a time-haunted land of mystery and evil in which the Western, modern way of life seemed to hold little sway. Things happened here. Inexplicably terrible things which were mentioned only in hushed whispers by frightened peasants.

With a nervous gulp, Myers plunged on into the darkness. There was nothing else for it.

He had only been going a couple of minutes when it started to rain. At first it was just a few drops but it soon became heavier. A sudden flash of lightning rent the murk asunder, illuminating the great straggling trees on either side. They were of a variety he had never seen before. Thunder boomed ominously in the distance.

Head down, hands thrust deep into his pockets, the leather case clenched tightly under one arm, Myers stubbornly walked on. Grimly, he squared his shoulders and gritted his teeth, his face set in a dripping scowl, his eyes sharp and alert. This had to be the worst assignment he had ever been on and it appeared that things were just going from bad to worse for, without any means of transport, short of his own feet, he was now deep in enemy territory. The more suspicious part of his mind could not help but entertain the idea that this entire mission had been a setup for what should have been a relatively easy task of procuring the secret documents had instead resulted in a bloody shootout necessitating his swift departure from Turkey. It was this belief that gave him the determination to keep going, in the full knowledge that if he were to discover just who was behind this then he would make them pay. Whatever it took.

An inner rage lent him strength and he began to jog, keen now to get out of the rain and find somewhere he could spend the night. He had passed numerous decrepit farmyard barns further back and he hoped that there might be some up ahead.

He stopped briefly in order to tie a shoe-lace. It was then that, back along the road he had travelled, he saw approaching headlights, the dull, yellow beams looking like the eyes of some alien monster. The vehicle was not travelling fast, indeed, as he crouched there watching it, he had the unnerving impression that the occupants were looking for him. Maybe his pursuers had discovered where he had crashed and were now trying to track him down.

Straining his eyes, Myers was sure that whoever was back there had brought the car to a standstill. Then, faintly, he heard the slamming of a door and the revving of an engine. The vehicle began to move towards him once more.

Knowing that there was little time to spare, Myers headed into the undergrowth. His marshy surroundings were hideously dark; a morass of stinking, dank pools on either side. He sank low into a patch of dense ferns, grasping his gun, aware of the heavy thumping of his heart.

The headlights drew closer, accompanied by the spluttering wheeze and the rattling of the approaching vehicle. It sounded as though it were on its last legs. Then it came to stop. A car door was opened, followed shortly after by another one. Two clearly agitated Bulgarian voices could be heard.

Myers knew nothing of the language, however it was fairly obvious that the others were keen to find him and that they would stop at nothing to retrieve the secret files that he had stolen. He didn't move, well aware that any sound he made would draw their attention. Cold water began to seep into his shoes and he realised with some alarm that he was slowly sinking into the brackish depths. Looking down, he could see that the water was now over his ankles. For some reason this foul dampness seemed to be something other than just a physical thing. It was almost as though the chill was spreading into his very soul.

Accompanied by a stream of harsh words, a beam of torch-light panned over to Myer's left. Countless seconds passed as he crouched on the damp ground, the horrendous stench of the marsh gases almost causing him to be sick. It seemed as though the mire was oozing over him, attempting to pull him down, to engulf him completely. No doubt men had been lost in these trackless swamps and once beneath these black waters, their bodies would never be recovered.

The voices ceased. With a sense of relief, Myers heard the car doors being slammed shut, the engine started up after several tries, and his pursuers drove off. From the sounds of it, they had decided to go back in the direction from whence they had come. It could be that they had considered it un-likely, given the state of the wrecked vehicle he had escaped from, that he could have got far.

Dragging himself out of the swamp, which was now up to his knees, Myers crawled his way back onto the road. He was soaked and he was stinking, but all that mattered was that he still had the files. He felt a sudden sharp pain in his leg. It was too dark to see things properly, however, reaching down with his hand he felt the slimy wetness of something slug-like adhered to his soaked trouser leg. Whether it was a leech or something else he didn't know but it had bitten through the thin fabric. Wincing, he squeezed its bloated body between his fingers, pulping it before painfully plucking it free. Run-ning his hands over his lower legs, he brushed off several more which hadn't as yet latched their puckered mouths onto his flesh.

How much longer would he have to go on before he reached anything that even remotely resembled civilisation? It could be all night. Maybe he would be better off finding shelter somewhere among the trees and resting until dawn.

That said, it was highly probable that his pursuers would widen their search for they had no doubt been given explicit orders to find him at all costs. It was just as vital for them to retrieve the classified documents as it was for him to hand them over to his superiors. And he knew from personal experience what failure could mean in this great game of global espionage.

Accompanied by the sound of his squelching shoes, Myers jogged along the road. He was drenched, cold and covered in filth. His sodden clothes clung to him like a sagging, second skin. At least it seemed as though the rain was beginning to slacken.

He stopped. Were those lights up ahead? Rubbing the dampness from his eyes, he peered in that direction. There was no doubt in his mind now. There were lights glowing less than a kilometre away over to his right. They appeared to be static—perhaps house lights. They seemed to be oil lamps as opposed to electric.

It was about time his fortune changed. Surely there would be someone there who could help him—whether willingly or unwillingly. That, of course, was for them to decide, however, removing the automatic from his pocket, he knew just how persuasive he could be if the situation warranted it. If he was lucky there would be a car or truck that he could make use of—some means of escaping from this godforsaken land.

Myers walked purposefully towards the lights. He had only gone several yards when he heard the faint music. He stopped and listened. The almost unearthly quality in the high-pitched whistling and in the wailing screech of violins sawed at his soul. The sound was unlike anything he had ever heard before although he had heard tales of the violently passionate wild gypsy music that the forgotten hillfolk still made. For some reason he could not help but feel that there was an *evilness* to the frantic playing; something which he couldn't define but was undeniably there.

Abruptly, the tempo changed and the music became eerily sombre. There was now a haunting, almost unholy edge to it. It was as though a nightmare had been made audible.

Myers was not one to scare easily and yet a ripple of fear threatened to momentarily overcome him. It was widely rumoured that the gypsies of this land; the Roma, the Kardarashi and the Vlach, were a fiercely xenophobic lot and that they held allegiance to none but themselves. They were also rumoured to be highly volatile, as capricious and tempestuous as the wilds from which they originated. If he had plenty of money on him he may have been able to bargain with them, but he knew the price of their assistance would be steep indeed.

Apprehensively, he began to walk forward once more, his nerves tingling. From the sounds of it there was quite a gathering and as he neared he was somewhat dismayed to notice a complete lack of parked vehicles. The building itself was slightly off the road and shrouded in gloom and as it began to emerge, spectrally, from the darkness, he could discern that it was at least three storeys tall with two smaller annexes. There was a general feeling of oddness about its design as though it was the product of some insane architect. He had been threading his way through the backwaters of Bulgaria for nigh on two days now and this was unlike any of the buildings he had seen previously.

Suddenly the hellish music stopped.

After a hasty look over his shoulder, Myers returned the gun to his pocket, ensuring it was within easy reach should things turn nasty. He waited the best part of a minute, still undecided as to whether engaging with these people would be a wise move. Perhaps he was being too paranoid, too cautious, after all it could be that these simple folk would prove to be helpful, providing they could understand anything of what he told them. There was only one way to find out.

The last thing he wanted was for attention to be drawn to the contents of the slim leather case he carried. Looking around, he saw a large tree, at the base of which he cleared away some of the thorny vegetation in order to deposit the secret files. Once satisfied that they were well concealed, he walked up to the main door, turned the handle and went inside.

Twenty or so wary faces turned towards him. They were a miserable and unfriendly-looking lot—their clothes, hands and faces covered in what looked like a month's amount of grime and dirt from working the fields. Most were short and stunted, long-haired and bearded, their unpleasant faces set in permanent scowls. From the doorway, Myers' initial reaction was to turn on his heels and make a run for it for there was a blatant animosity levelled at him. He was the outsider and he had dared walk into this social gathering uninvited. Mustering his courage, he defiantly stood his ground and glanced around, taking in his surroundings. The room itself was extremely run-down; the wallpaper peeling away in great flakes, the floor unswept and the black-beamed ceiling sagged noticeably.

It was clear that the building served as a tavern or an inn of some sort for several unsavoury patrons we gathered at a makeshift bar. Others were sat at tables, whilst in one corner a group of bizarre-looking musicians glared at him. There was a fat, drooling imbecile seated at a dust-covered piano and a tall, gangly freak cradling an ancient-looking double bass. Mercifully shadowed, something unsightly with a violin sat huddled in a corner.

There was not a single woman to be seen, which, given the overall level of ugliness of those inside was probably for the best.

A gruff, questioning Bulgarian voice called out from behind the bar.

Myers shook his head. "I don't understand."

The man who had spoken stepped forward. "You English, yes?" He smiled in a tight, wintry way, with the smile never reaching his eyes. He was tall and broad-shouldered, with a thick, high-bridged nose and eyes set a little too close to it, giving him a mean, crafty look.

Myers nodded. "Yes. I had an accident on the road." He was becoming increasingly uncomfortable under the disturbing scrutiny he was being subjected to.

The stranger stomped over and grinned, revealing a largely toothless mouth. With what was supposed to be a friendly gesture, he patted Myers painfully hard on the shoulder and steered him towards an empty table. "You need a room? Food and a good drink, yes?" He gestured towards a stool. "You sit here."

Myers sat down, positioning himself so that he had his back to a wall. Gazing around, he found it hard not to stare back at the gathered misfits. With some level of revulsion, he noted a badly scarred hydrocephalic giggling as he shared his supper with a large rat that squatted at the end of his plate.

"You like soup? I make great soup." Without waiting for an answer, the innkeeper slouched off behind the bar and went through a door into what was presumably the kitchen.

With some level of relief, Myers noted that he was no longer the main focus of attention. What he needed right now was an opportunity to get out of these wet clothes, take a warm shower and have a good night's sleep. He was considering the wisdom of asking whether or not there was a room available and thus risk spending the night here when, out of the corner of his eye, he detected someone coming towards him.

It was the gaunt man he had seen with the double bass.

The musician pulled up a stool and sat down. He had a long, drooping moustache, which seemed to dominate his face, although it could not quite detract from the cross-eyed stare that, in its own, strange way, regarded Myers suspiciously. "Nikolai." He pointed to himself.

"Hello." Myers tried to smile, to at least present a veneer of friendliness. However, he could not help but feel uncomfortable about all of this. He watched as Nikolai scratched at his moustache. There was a bad stink coming from the other and when the man grinned he revealed a set of front teeth which were sharp and crooked.

Several uneasy minutes passed, neither of the two initiating any conversation. Eventually the innkeeper returned carrying a tray on which rested a mug of beer and a bowl of steaming soup.

Nodding thankfully, Myers started on the soup, pleased to be doing something to break the awkward silence. He spat out the first mouthful. It was truly horrendous, but whereas his displeasure ought to have earned a comment or an apology, it got no reaction whatsoever from the innkeeper. It was almost as though he had expected this.

Flicking a large beetle off the table, the grin on Nikolai's face widened.

The soup had left a foul aftertaste in his mouth, prompting Myers to take a hearty glug of beer. It was surprisingly nice. Cool and refreshing. He had now made up his mind that as soon as it was finished he would get away from here and its unusual clientele. To hell with staying here the night. He would much rather take his chances out in the wilderness. He took another drink, aware that the innkeeper was watching him speculatively.

And then, over the innkeeper's shoulder, Myers saw the front door open. Two men in dark black coats stood for a moment, menacingly framed in the doorway. He could tell just from their appearance that they were some of the thugs who were after him. Lowering his head, he tried to look inconspicuous, to melt in with the weirdos.

The enemy agents got the same kind of reception that he had received only minutes before. All eyes turned to stare at them. One of the men in the doorway said something in an authoritative voice.

For one dreadful moment Myers was certain that someone was going to give him away. His fingers tightened on the gun in his pocket, ready to draw it out and start shooting but after a few more words the door was slammed shut and the men were gone.

The innkeeper walked over. "Those men…after you? They say they will be on the lookout for you. Maybe best to stay here tonight."

"Thanks for not telling them that I was here." It appeared that Myers had misjudged these people. Clearly looks could be deceptive. Maybe these outcasts felt some kindred spirit for someone on the run from the authorities. "So I take it you have a spare room?" he asked.

* * * *

Myers came awake swiftly and sharply, that part of his mind which had learned never to fully sleep dragging him back to consciousness at the faintest flicker of sound. For a long moment, he lay there on the low wooden bed, searching the darkness with eyes and ears, straining to pick up the sound that had woken him, to identify it and pinpoint its location.

Then it came again—the faint sound of someone moving just outside the door to his room. As always, before going to bed in a strange place, he had left his holstered gun propped by the bedstead, where it could be reached readily. His right hand grasped the butt. Wearing only a rather ragged nightshirt and a pair of breeches which had been loaned by the innkeeper, he rose to his feet, his eyes staring fixedly, almost cat-like, at the door. Hurriedly he put his shoes on.

Myers had locked the door before settling down for the night; a precaution he always took when staying indoors in foreign parts, but from the sounds of it, someone else had a spare key. It turned in the lock and he heard the handle twist. A moment passed before the door slowly creaked open. Through narrowed eyes, he caught a glimpse of the faint light from the corridor outside, shining around the edge of the door. Stealthily, he sidestepped to his right, clinging to the shadows of the room, making for the space behind where the door would open.

The door opened wider and a figure edged inside. He could see it was Nikolai. Cautiously, the man crept in further, his footsteps barely audible. A faint gleam of lamplight on the knife he carried announced his intention—leaving Myers in no doubt that this was something other than a social call. Swiftly, he moved forward and crashed the butt of the automatic down on the skull of his early morning intruder.

Uttering a curse, the man staggered back, falling to his knees under the force of the blow. He lunged forward, arms flailing, head down, pummelling into Myers as he pushed himself upright, catching him before he could crack down a second time. Together they fell back, colliding with a chair and falling to the floor, both the automatic and the knife spiralling out of the melee.

Scrambling to his feet, Myers grabbed the other by the shirt collar and was just about to smash his right fist into the moustachioed face when Nikolai jabbed him in the stomach. There was a dull roaring in his ears and all the wind seemed to rush out of his lungs. An uppercut from Nikolai sent Myers staggering back, his head temporarily swimming.

Nikolai pulled back into the dingy corridor. Hate swelled in his piggish eyes.

Myers had been trained to fight and kill if need be. Both were things he was good at. Springing forward, he caught hold of one of Nikolai's arms and hauled him close. With his other hand, he reached out and grabbed a handful of unwashed hair. He slammed the head down to meet his rising knee.

Howling in pain, Nikolai tried to break free, smacking two quick-fire jabs into Myers' ribs, savagely breaking the hold. Then, even as Myers was about to chop down with the palm of his right hand, Nikolai pulled back, spotting the shadowy outline of his knife on the floor. Clambering swiftly over the bed he whisked it up. Myers was on him before he could take a swing, barging him into the wall, crushing the air from him and knocking the blade from his hand. Viciously, he then hauled his attacker to his feet and spun him around, driving his head into the wall before throwing the badly battered man to the floor. For a moment, he considered standing on the other's throat, but changed his mind and bent down to retrieve his gun. It was that moment's indecision that allowed Nikolai to act. With a twist of his boot, he tripped Myers up, sending him falling against the bed.

Before Myers could get to his feet, his attacker was on him, punching and scratching. Fighting savagely, the two tore at each other, each seeking to get in the one blow that would assure victory—whether a kick in the groin or a gouge in the eye. Blood streamed from a gash on Nikolai's forehead and dripped down onto Myers' face.

Bloodlust lent Nikolai strength. His hands clasped around Myers' throat, the nails digging in and puncturing the soft flesh. His grip tightened and Myers now began to panic. Desperately, he reached out for anything that might be useful, his fingers tightening around the handle of a ceramic jug. He crashed it down on the head of his attacker, succeeding in forcing the other off. Gasping for air, he groggily got to his feet and half-fell out into the corridor.

With a maniacal scream Nikolai came charging, arms outstretched, curling a little, fingers stiff, as if he already had his foe in the circle of his arms, crushing him in a bear hug. Myers stepped to one side and drove in two solid punches, both landing hard and firm on the other's jaw, Nikolai's forward momentum adding weight and force to them. His head danced loosely on his shoulders and his knees began to buckle, took a surge of strength, then went completely as a third jab from Myers burst his nose.

Nikolai slumped to the floor, out for the count.

Rubbing his wounds, Myers went back into the room and retrieved his automatic. So much for Bulgarian hospitality, he thought. Stepping back onto the landing, he froze. Something strange was happening to the man on the ground. He was shaking terribly, convulsing as though he was undergoing an epileptic fit. Squealing like a skewered pig, he started to undergo a gruesome transformation. Greyish-black hair sprouted from his hands and face. His eyes narrowed and turned pinkish. His ears became pointed and his nose became a whiskered snout. His mouth was stretched back, snaggle-toothed incisors emerging from his gums. Inch-long ragged nails tore through the flesh of his fingers.

With a snarl, the thing that had been Nikolai scrambled to its feet.

"*Jesus Christ!*" Myers stepped back in utter shock. What in God's name was this?

Hissing its wrath, the thing approached. It was slightly smaller than the human version of Nikolai had been, is back hunched, clawed hands extended, ready to rend.

Myers raised his gun and shot off half a dozen bullets. The force of the slugs knocked the horror back but did not seem to cause any true damage. He had heard stories and seen films of men who had turned into wolves, immune to everything bar silver bullets. Could it be that this was such a creature? He fired twice more, then sprang back into his room and slammed the door to, hastily dragging a chair over and ramming it against the handle.

There came a loud thump on the door and the wood rattled.

Myers had to get out of here. For the moment, his survival instincts were greater than his fear. He dashed for the thick curtains and parted them, lifted the window and looked down.

The door was thumped a second time and one of the wooden boards splintered. With the thing's third blow its clawed hand smashed through the door.

Myers had no more bullets. Nerves afire, he clambered out of the window, took a hold of the lintel and let himself drop. A second or two later, the ground came up to meet him, the impact jarring through his feet, up his legs and into his entire body. He lost his footing and fell over backwards. For a moment, the pain in his ankles was excruciating, but at least he hadn't broken anything.

The hideous face was at the window, peering down, snout twitching, its red-rimmed eyes full of hatred.

Gritting his teeth, Myers scrambled to his feet. What the hell was going on? He turned and began limping away into the darkness, his heart sinking as he heard a chorus of angry shouts coming from around the corner of the tavern.

A crowd of dark shapes came into view. Some held aloft flaming brands. There were far too many of them to fight. One of their number rushed forward. He was a thoroughly ugly individual; bearded and with shoulders that were nearly as broad as he was tall. Laughing insanely, he leapt at Myers, tackling him to the ground. Then there came kicks and punches. A black hood was savagely forced over his head and something hard smote against it, knocking him out.

* * * *

"*Psst!* You. Englishman. Are you alive?"

Myers began to stir. From somewhere within the gloom, he heard a whispered voice, the words heavily accented. Pain crept into his body, letting him know that he was very much alive, although for how much longer, he had no idea. His head ached and it was with a considerable effort and a wrenching of neck muscles that he managed to look to one side. Panic set in as he felt the cold dampness at his back and he realised that he was manacled to a wall; arms outstretched. He saw the flash of torchlight. A moment later there came the sound of a metal gate opening and suddenly a dark figure appeared.

"I don't know who these people are that have you prisoner and to be honest, I don't care, but if you don't tell me where they've taken the files I'll kill you where you stand."

In the dim light, Myers could see that the man who had spoken was tall and well-built. His black hair was parted down the middle. His features were strong and chiselled, with a jutting jaw and wide forehead. A deep scar ran down his right cheek. He was one of the men whom he had seen enter the tavern; one of those that had been searching for him—one of the enemy agents.

From further back in the shadows came an agitated whisper which prompted the big man to turn around. He responded in Bulgarian before glaring at Myers once more. Menacingly, he drew out a knife, its blade serrated.

"I know where the files are. Get me out of here and I'll show you." Myers knew his situation was dire to say the least and that this was his only card left to play. Throughout his career as a professional spy he had not once been captured by the enemy yet he was fully aware of the many means of interrogation that were commonly used. He didn't think this man was a professional however, rather he was an underling, a bit of hired muscle. If it had been someone with the proper skill and training he would have been in serious trouble.

"Tell me where they are!"

"You're going to have to get me out of here first."

The big man held his knife against Myers' neck. "Tell me or I'll cut your throat."

"Do that and you'll never find them."

The man's companion who had been stationed by the cell door skulked into view. He was shorter, timid-looking, bespectacled. His eyes were darting in all directions and it was obvious that he wanted to be gone from this place as soon as possible. He gestured animatedly as he spoke as quietly as he could to the other in his own language, a gun in his hand.

The big man snorted his displeasure at something. He then returned his knife to a belt sheath and turned his attention to the shackles that held Myers. With an audible click, the lock which held his left hand sprang open. The tall thug moved into position and began to pick the remaining manacle. When he couldn't get it to open, he gave a grunt and with a superhuman effort wrestled it from the wall.

"Thanks," Myers said coolly. Had he been feeling up to it he might have considered taking a swing at his liberator, using the length of chain that now dangled from his right wrist as a weapon. Before he could make such a foolhardy move, a vice-like hand clamped down on his shoulder and he was roughly steered forward, out of the cell.

The man with the gun led the way along a dank stretch of passage before arriving at a flight of stone steps that went up to a small door. A terrible smell struck the backs of their nostrils, their feet splashing through the small puddles that had gathered on the ground. Rats scurried along the tunnel and Myers couldn't help but notice the strange way in which the large rodents seemed to be paying acute attention to their movements.

The door on the short landing was opened and in the torch-light Myers could see that he was in a large cavern that looked like an abandoned mine. Heaps of rubble and collapsed roof supports lay on the ground and nearby there was a sprawl of thick and rusty metal chains along with some huge cogs and dented buckets. More chains dangled from the cavern roof. In the centre, some piece of long-forgotten mining machinery lay broken and twisted, its rusted components resembling a giant, upturned, multi-legged insect. Over to their right, a further passage wound its way elsewhere and to their left, a tunnel-like ramp descended into the unlit depths. Directly opposite them, against one wall, was a rickety, wooden ladder.

"Move it!"

Myers was viciously pushed forward.

The smaller Bulgarian stopped suddenly, his eyes wide like those of a frightened rabbit's behind his thick lenses. He muttered something and pulled a chain with a small crucifix on it from beneath his collar.

Myers knew the other was scared and what was more, given what he had seen Nikolai transform into, he had good reason to be so. He too was frightened. The fear was like an unreachable prickling between his shoulder blades; a cold heat that raised sweat to his forehead. Now that the three of them had stopped he could detect sounds, barely audible sounds, like the burrowing of worms as heard by someone buried alive in a coffin or the fluttering of birds heard by someone drowning in a pool. The sounds grew louder. And now he was sure of both the source and the cause. *Rats*…scampering up the ramp, streaming from the deeps—a whole pattering, verminous horde, hungry for blood and eager for flesh.

Suddenly, out of the darkness they came—a plague of rats and a dark tide of misshapen grotesques; their faces twisted and repellent, their peasant clothes torn and filthy. Some brandished primitive weapons—sticks, knives and sickles—but most of the score or so were unarmed, their teeth and claws more than compensating. Several hunched, scabrous horrors rushed forward, their hideous faces and whiskered snouts matted with blood and dirt no doubt gathered from a lifetime of looting graveyards and gnawing on corpses.

As one, the three men screamed and rushed for the ladder.

Myers got there first and started to frantically pull himself up. His limbs ached and his mind was a riot of thoughts. The ladder went up maybe forty feet or so, ending at a stout trapdoor lid. Hanging on with one hand, he pushed with all of his might and it mercifully swung open. Pale yellow sunlight bathed the wrecked room into which he scrambled, temporarily stinging his eyes. He turned, tempted for a moment to slam the lid shut on the two ascending Bulgarians. When he saw the gun the shorter man had levelled at him he changed his mind and pulled back further, permitting the other to climb free.

And then came a loud, splintering crack followed by bloodcurdling screams.

Heart thumping, Myers watched as the small man glanced down the trapdoor, noting the way in which the other winced as though he had been a spectator to something extremely gruesome. Myers assumed from the other's reaction and the noises he had heard, that the ladder had given way causing the big man to fall into the midst of the bestial degenerates. The remaining Bulgarian slammed the wooden lid down. At least those horrors wouldn't be climbing up.

"Now then, Mr. Myers, let me introduce myself," the man said, panting from the exertion of the climb. "My name is Dragomir Sarac."

Myers was thrown by the man's perfect English and the use of his name.

"The agency I work for is very keen to acquire those files that were stolen from our research station. So much so that I am prepared to make you a deal. Unless you were just—as you English say—'saving your bacon' back in the cell, you claim to know where they are. If you hand them over to me I *may* let you live." Sarac's face was as cold as his voice.

"*You may let me live?*" Myers said incredulously. "I think it more likely that we're both going to die here." He found it hard to believe how this man could still be so calm after what had just happened. Right now he couldn't give a damn about the top-secret data. All he wanted was to get as far from here as possible. There were things under their very feet that had no right to be. Surely even the shadowy world of national allegiance and covert operations went by the wayside when faced with this. They should be uniting to stamp out this abomination, this threat to civilised existence, instead of continuing in their game of cloak and dagger.

"Unlike Krastio," Sarac crossed himself, "I knew exactly what was going on here. I am of the Roma and we have come to live with such things."

A fresh wave of unreality pounded at Myers. "You know about these monsters?"

"They are the *vrkolak*—the shadow men. Vampire-like shapeshifters, creatures born of nightmare. I recognised them the moment I saw them. Even in their human forms they are discernible to one who knows what to look for. Their shadows are darker than yours or mine. It is daylight now and they will not willingly venture outside. For the time being they will retreat to their lairs, bury themselves in their underground warrens. They are as old as the land. Their skeletons are sometimes unearthed, found staked down with iron rods."

There was a question Myers had to ask. "Why did they take me prisoner? Why didn't they kill me?"

"Simply because you are very fortunate. Tonight is the night when the moon is at its darkest. It is tonight that you were to be offered to the matriarch of this clan."

"You knew all this…and yet you still came down to free me."

"As I said, I want those files. Besides, I have my own protection. The crucifix I carry will keep most of them at bay."

Myers wanted out of here. The room was becoming oppressive and there was a bad stench rising up through the trapdoor. "Come on then. I'll show you where I've hidden the documents." With the gun trained on him, he headed for the door, opened it and stepped outside.

The early morning sunlight was weak but welcome. Myers noted with some surprise that he was actually only a couple of hundred yards away from the building which he took to be the tavern from which he had escaped earlier that morning. He had only seen it in the darkness but he was fairly sure it was the one. Parked over to one side he saw a car, no doubt the one in which the two agents had travelled here in.

"Believe me, I won't hesitate to shoot you," Sarac warned. "What's more, I won't kill you. I'll just cripple you and leave you here. Leave you here for the matriarch. Think about that before you try anything."

"How do I know you won't just shoot me after I take you to them?"

"I guess you'll just have to take my word."

"Hmm. Thought as much." With the manacle still dangling from his right wrist, Myers began walking towards the tree near which he had secreted the black case. As he headed over, he couldn't help but think that perhaps one of those foul beings had seen him hide it there and had then stolen it. How would he explain that away to Sarac? Thankfully, it was still there. He pointed down at it. "They're all inside."

"Get it!" Sarac gestured with the gun.

Carefully, Myers went down on one knee and retrieved the case.

"Now open it. Let me see."

Myers opened the container, revealing the highly sought after papers.

"Excellent. Now place it at your feet and walk over there."

Myers knew what was going to come next. This bastard was going to execute him, shoot him dead where he stood. With a cry, he threw the case at the other and leapt to one side, swinging out with the chain attached to his arm. It whipped across Sarac's hand, knocking the gun to the ground.

Sarac had been disarmed but he now had the case. He clutched it to his chest as he pulled back, staying out of reach of Myers' swings.

Spotting the fallen gun, Myers crouched down in order to get it. He picked it up, aware that the small Bulgarian had already taken to his heels. The man was fast, sprinting as though all the devils in Hell were after him.

Myers had never been keen on shooting someone in the back but he was prepared to make an exception. He took aim and squeezed the trigger.

The bullet took Sarac in the lower left leg. Limping, he staggered off course. Realising he wasn't going to reach the car before another shot hit him he half-fell, half-ran towards the tavern door.

Myers fired again, cursing as the bullet smashed into the crumbling white-washed wall an inch above Sarac's head. A third shot tore into the door. And then his target had disappeared inside.

All was eerily quiet.

Checking the gun, Myers saw that there were three bullets remaining. He now had one hell of a decision to make. Common sense screamed at him to get in the car, hotwire it if the keys hadn't been left in the ignition and get out of here; or, venture back into that horrible place, kill Sarac and retrieve the files.

Now that he had the time to take notice, he shuddered as he gazed at the decrepit building and its surroundings. Daylight did nothing to mask the fact that this place was evil—it was almost as tangible as the ground beneath his feet or the chill mistiness in the air. Whatever wickedness had been perpetrated in this foul place had left an unholy residue; a lingering trace of vile corruption which, alongside the memories of what he had seen, was enough to make the skin crawl.

Still, he had the gun. And hadn't Sarac said that these things would stay underground during the day? Maybe the enemy agent was even now lying bleeding to death in the main room, in which case it would only take a minute or two to finish him off and retrieve the papers. Didn't he owe it to those others who had died back in Istanbul?

Myers cursed. Mustering his courage, he moved forward, gun held out before him as though it were a talisman which would keep the darkness at bay. At the doorway, he could see the main communal area much as he had left it that evening, the tables set as though in readiness for another evening's gypsy revel—in addition to the odd little bit of abduction, attempted murder and shape-changing skulduggery. Apart from that, it was dark and empty. Fresh blood stains lay spattered on the floor.

He made his way in. In the gloom, he could just make out the bar and the door beyond. To his right, around the corner was where the stairs up to the first floor began. After a brief pause, during which he wrestled the mental image of the dreadful horde from his mind, he made his way over to the foot of the stairs. Looking down, he could see more blood. Sarac had definitely gone this way. Treading carefully, aware of the many shadowy shapes, he edged forward, his body pressed tightly against the wall.

Before him the stairs ascended into the gloom.

Myers found it hard to look up, to push his vision into the darkness. In his mind, he could see the many sets of red eyes that peered out from the shadows.

There came a creak from overhead.

That same cold prickling that he had felt inside the mine crept unwelcomingly up his back. Slowly, he started up the stairs, afraid now that each step would fall on a rotten tread and that he would crash through into a dark cellar where he would soon find himself surrounded by thousands of flesh-hungry monsters.

The sound came again, the unnerving creak of tortured wood. It sounded like either a clumsy step on a loose board or the slow rocking of an old-fashioned chair. This was becoming truly nightmarish. The hand which grasped the gun was shaking and the desire to just turn around and flee was almost overwhelming.

Somehow, Myers kept moving, trying his best to convince himself that there were no bogeymen lurking under the floorboards or grotesques ready to spring out of the dark places.

In the shadowy darkness, he reached the top of the stairs and started along the corridor. The door to the room at the far end, the one in which he had spent the night was wide open. The creaking was coming from this room and it was here the trail of blood led.

What madness drove him forward he would never know. Stepping out into the doorway he peered inside.

Shadows shifted, drawn back towards one corner, as though to conceal further the ragged form that sat huddled in its rocking chair, absently flicking through the contents of the file. It was a horrid thing, an ancient, wizened being, wrapped in a tattered shawl, its greenish, furry arms wiry, its face more shrivelled and rat-like than any of the others—apart from the brass-rimmed pince-nez it had resting on its whiskered snout. Its pink-red eyes were rheumy and burned with an intense malevolence. It was festooned with dusty amulets and terrible gypsy trinkets.

Uttering unholy curses, the matriarch of the *vrkolak*—a *veshtitsi*, an ancient, vampire-witch—rose arthritically from her chair.

"God save me!" At point-blank range, Myers fired his remaining three bullets into it. It was only then that he saw the battered and bloody form of Sarac lying in one corner. He was still alive, the impotent crucifix warped and blackened at his feet.

The horror slavered and spat, the bullet wounds closing up and vanishing.

Knowing there was nothing else for it, Myers snatched the file from the fiend's claws and ran out of the room. Several of the papers went astray but he was past caring. If and when he returned to England he would retire from espionage. Become a postman or something. To think that he would have been offered to this horrendous thing sent an uncontrollable shudder of revulsion through him. He lost his footing and tumbled down the stairs. On hands and knees he crawled out of the tavern into the sunlight dreading at the last moment that he would feel the thing grasp him and pull him back inside; into the shadow-filled interior.

Desperately, Myers stumbled towards the car. He stopped and peered back at the upper storey windows with their thick curtains trying not to imagine what horrible fate lay in store for Sarac. Had there been any bullets left he would have shot the Bulgarian, as an act of mercy. Throwing the case onto the passenger seat, he set about fiddling with the wires. The engine sparked into life and he was reversing out. Soon he was speeding away as yet unaware of the two puncture marks on his neck just below his collar.

A PRESENCE OF EVIL

Having been forced to take their own lives they were now back for revenge.

"Please, Inspector, do take a seat."

"I'm no longer in the police. I retired several years ago, so let's dispense with the title, shall we?" Saffin said, easing himself back into a chair. "Call me Robert." He was a relatively plump, white-haired man in his late sixties. Taking a glance around, he was surprised at just how 'normal' his surroundings were. He had expected the room to be adorned with mystical-themed furnishings; a hand-of-glory on the mantelpiece, a poster of Eliphas Levi's drawing of Baphomet on a wall, Ouija boards and skull-candles. There wasn't even a pack of tarot cards to be seen.

"Very well, Robert. How can I help?"

Saffin thought for a moment as he looked at the man seated opposite; a man who went by the name of John Cornelius, although, having done his research the last time their paths had crossed, he knew that his real name was John Harvey. Cornelius certainly sounded better for the line of work he was in—paranormal investigation. Saffin guessed he must have been about fifty and he knew that not only was he an expert on the occult but he also had over a dozen successful exorcisms to his credit, all conducted privately, outside the jurisdiction of the Church. "Several years ago I was called out to what, certainly at the time, was believed to be a multiple murder scene. It was at Carrin-Bridge Manor. You may have read something about it in the papers."

Cornelius shook his head. "Sorry, can't say that I have."

"Well, I must say that doesn't really surprise me. That's because what I discovered there was, to a large extent, covered up with only a tiny snippet of information given to the press."

"Sounds intriguing."

"Yes, it is." Saffin pulled gently at his bottom lip. He had deliberated for the past several months on whether or not he should seek outside help for the problems he was facing and it had taken both time and courage to get this far. Now that he was actually here and about to confide in someone about what was troubling him, he wasn't sure how to proceed. "Anyway, I'll try to be concise. Carrin-Bridge Manor had been used as a base of operations by a violent criminal gang from one of the roughest parts of Tyneside. Their leader was the notorious Jimmy Darlington who was wanted for countless crimes; murder, armed robbery, torture, drug smuggling. You name it, Darlington was involved. The man was a vicious, psychopathic sadist. A real nasty piece of work."

Cornelius had just finished pouring two small whiskies. He handed one over. "Now that you've mentioned Darlington, I do seem to recall something about the story. Yes, wasn't there a siege at his hideout resulting in his death?"

"Not exactly. I was one of the first on the scene and although we had the place surrounded I could tell that Darlington wasn't going to put up any resistance. After numerous warnings for them to come out peacefully it was decided that we should go in." Saffin took a sip of his whisky. "We stormed the place but not a single gunshot was fired. You see, Darlington and the other four members of his outfit were already dead. Darlington was found in the main hall, hanging from the balcony. The others were found in various rooms—one of them with cut wrists in the bathroom; another was in an upstairs bedroom, having blown his head off with a shotgun, his brains plastered to the ceiling. All had obviously been dead for some time."

"They'd all taken their own lives?"

"Apparently."

"Very strange."

Saffin gave a half-hearted smile. "It gets stranger. For many years Carrin-Bridge lay abandoned. I guess the place had gained something of a reputation, for although only a handful of people knew what had actually happened there it soon became common knowledge that it had been used for some form of criminal activity. Anyway, at the beginning of last year, a family moved in. Americans. Fairly wealthy folk who either had no knowledge about the manor's past or weren't all that bothered by it. However, a few months back, I started to get nightmares—or rather visions—in which their young son seemed to be trying to talk to me, to warn me about something going on in the house, of some evil returning."

"And, have you been back since? Have you spoken to this child or his parents?"

"Yes. I drove out there yesterday. His name's Dominic." Saffin shivered at some bad memory. "His father was away for the day but his mother received me openly enough, but it was an awkward meeting as you can no doubt imagine. Now, I don't profess to being sensitive to ghosts or anything like that but whilst I was there I was aware of a presence. It was like a cold shadow clinging to me all the time."

"And the boy, Dominic. Did he recognise *you*?"

"No. Although it's definitely him I've seen in my dreams. Without doubt."

"Hmm. Very interesting." It was getting quite dim in the room so Cornelius rose from his chair and switched the lights on.

"I've been giving it all some thought and the only thing I can think of is that the place is haunted. What concerns me is that whatever evil entity lurks there, no doubt the same thing that caused Darlington and his men to kill themselves, may be about to attack that innocent family, starting with the boy. I've come to you seeking your assistance in this matter."

Saffin tried to imagine just what sort of a team they would make. Him, the ex-detective; podgy and pushing on seventy, and the paranormal investigator; urbane and with a certain boyish, handsome look to his face despite his mature years.

Cornelius sat down and crossed his legs. "I'll obviously help as best I can. I'll make a start by consulting some of my books to see if I can track down anything regarding Carrin-Bridge Manor. Once I've done that I think we should go out there together so that I can, providing that the current owners are amenable, take a look around the property for myself. See if I can pick up any of the psychic emanations that you say you've experienced. What concerns me, Robert, is that we could be dealing with an incredibly powerful and evil entity. If it possesses the ability to drive five men to take their own lives then we shall have to be extremely cautious in our investigations."

* * * *

The next morning the two of them set off, Saffin doing the driving whilst Cornelius pored over some of the books he had brought. Prior to starting the hour-long journey, Saffin had made a call to the manor, hoping to be able to speak to its owners, inform them that they were coming, but he hadn't been able to get hold of anyone. There was no doubt that this was going to be tricky and that things had to be handled very delicately. *How exactly did one go about explaining something like this?* An inner doubt had plagued him since getting up that morning, gnawing away inside, making him question whether or not he was doing the right thing. It was only his belief that the boy could well be in danger that bolstered his resolution.

"Now here's something interesting." Cornelius tapped the page of the book he had open before him and began to read from it. "Carrin-Bridge Manor lays claim to being one of the oldest houses in England. Not only is it mentioned in the Domesday Book but much of its stonework allegedly comes from a Second Century Roman settlement named *Dugubris Maxiatus*. Allegedly, because no trace of this Roman site has ever been found, however there are tenuous links with Mithraic cult activity. There's no fixed date given for its construction. Over the centuries the house has been the country seat of several prominent aristocratic families and in the late Seventeenth Century one wing was converted into a privately run hospital by the owner at the time, a Reverend William Cavendish, a renowned physician and philanthropist who bequeathed much of his fortune to providing care for the sick and infirm."

"No mention of any ghosts or anything supernatural?"

"Doesn't seem to be but from my own experience in these matters that counts for nothing."

Saffin had brought the car to a stop at a set of traffic lights. They turned green and he stepped on the accelerator. "In the case of Darlington and his men, do you think that they all committed suicide at the same moment?"

"Quite possibly. And I don't mind telling you, Robert, but it's this that scares me."

Saffin threw his passenger a sideways glance. "Would you care to explain?"

"As I said before, I think that we're soon going to encounter something extremely wicked, something that has the power to drive a man, or in this case, *men*, to self-destruction. And I think it did this by getting into the minds of each of them. Like a disease almost."

Saffin gulped. Deep down a part of him shared a similar view but to have it confirmed by someone who was an expert in the field was unnerving. The thought that something could invade his private thoughts, take control of his mind and make him do the unthinkable was truly terrifying. And what was worse, he didn't know how such a thing could be prevented.

The rest of the journey passed in an uneasy silence as both men mentally wrestled with what dangers might possibly lie in store.

Carrin-Bridge Manor loomed before them, impressively, yet forlornly, silhouetted against the grey, late November morning sky. Architecturally, the walls were built of squared and coursed rubble with freestone and ashlar dressing no doubt built around the ancient Roman stones. The north front that they were now approaching comprised a central three-storey late Thirteenth Century pele tower with a taller circular stair turret and two-storey ranges which linked it to the left and a four bay servant's wing of three storeys to the right. Double chamfered mullion windows on the ground floor, a crenulated roof and copious coverings of ivy all added to its antiquated charm.

Saffin brought the car to a sudden halt. He could see Dominic sat on a swing in the garden, lazily pushing himself back and forth. There was a mischievous look on the dark-haired child's face.

"I take it that's Dominic?" Now that they had arrived, Cornelius slung his books into the back seat.

"Yes. Come on, let's see if we're going to be made welcome." Saffin unfastened his seatbelt and got out of the car. "Hello Dominic."

Suddenly a well-built man appeared from around the side of the building pushing a wheelbarrow laden with twigs and fallen leaves. "Yes? Can I help you?" From his accent it was obvious that he was American. "Say, you're not the guy that was here a day or so ago, are you?"

Dominic rushed over to join his father. "That's him, Daddy. He's a bad man. Tell him to go away."

"Nonsense. Now why don't you run along and play." The man turned to his visitors as the child ran off. "Please, don't mind my son." The American extended a hand which Saffin, and then Cornelius shook. "The name's Simon Walther. Do come in. Louise, that's my wife, and Dominic have been telling me all about you. About how you think the house might be haunted. Sounds great. To tell you the truth it's one of the main reasons I chose this place." He talked in a cheery, exuberant manner.

"You're not afraid of ghosts then, I take it?" asked Cornelius, following behind as the owner led them inside. He had just crossed the threshold when he felt a fleeting icy grasp at his chest. Looking up he suddenly caught a glimpse—nothing more than that—of a shadowy form dangling over the staircase. It vanished in the space of a heartbeat.

"*Me?* No way. Not that I've ever seen one of them." Walther led them into a richly-furnished study. "Make yourselves comfortable guys whilst I go fix us some drinks. My, those folks back in Baltimore are going to turn green with envy when I tell them I met some genuine English ghost-hunters." With that, he turned and left the room, calling out loudly for his wife.

Saffin saw Dominic briefly peer around the edge of the door. Then the boy had gone.

"Robert. I saw and felt something the moment I entered the hall," said Cornelius.

"You did!?"

"Yes. I think I saw the ghost of Darlington, or rather a residual trace he's left behind. There's no doubt in my mind that there's something here, that this place *is* haunted."

"It never occurred to me that Darlington would haunt this place. Although I suppose it makes some sense but it doesn't explain what caused the multiple suicides. There must be something here, something else which—"

Before Saffin could finish, Walther came bounding into the study. "My wife's going to bring the drinks in a minute." He sat down, a broad, enthusiastic smile on his face. It was the look of a child who had suddenly been given the best birthday present imaginable. "This is amazing. It really is."

"I'd hate to dampen your spirits, Mr. Walther, but I think it would be for the best if you were to take these matters a little less flippantly. There are powers here in this house that are both malign and dangerous." His rather melodramatic warning given, Cornelius returned from the bookshelf he was standing by and sank into a padded armchair.

Perversely, Walther was loving this. "Bring them on." He looked directly at the paranormal investigator. "Say, can you make them appear, so that we can seem them? Can you perform something like a séance? I often used Ouija boards when I was at college back in the States and we used to—"

"This is not a game, Mr. Walther! It is deadly serious… and we've reason to believe that your son may be involved," said Saffin.

"*Dominic?* In what way?" Walther asked concernedly.

"Has Dominic been having any nightmares of late?" Cornelius inquired.

"Not that I'm aware of." At that moment Mrs. Walther entered the study carrying a tray of drinks. "Has Dominic mentioned anything to you about having any nightmares?" he asked his wife.

"No. Hello again." Mrs. Walther gave Saffin a nervous smile and a wave. "I'll get him if you like so that you can ask him."

"That won't be necessary at the moment," said Cornelius. "But if I may, I'd like to take a look around your house. Would that be all right with you?"

Walther nodded. "Sure. But why don't you have your coffee and tell me a bit more about what you think's going on here first."

* * * *

It took Cornelius just over an hour to establish the exact locations where each of the gang members had met their ends, their unearthly residues detectable to one such as he. It had been a ghastly investigation, going from room to room, searching for what he termed 'cold spots,' focusing when he found one, trying to make contact. The messages that he was getting from the spirit world were garbled; some were filled with rage and wickedness, coming through in dreadful, soul-burning shades of coal-black and blood-red, whilst others were *purer*, whiter almost, imbued with a sense of benevolence, of innocence. There was a schism—a dark versus light conflict taking place. But he could tell that this transcendental equilibrium was out of balance, for the dark outnumbered, and out-powered, the light.

It was as he was leaving one of the upstairs bedrooms, one in which one of Darlington's men had overdosed on a copious amount of narcotics, that he felt the spectral hands at his throat.

Struggling to draw breath, Cornelius staggered against a wall. He broke into a coughing fit, his face turning red. His eyes were watering.

Saffin rushed to his aid.

Mercifully, the psychic attack was fleeting.

Cornelius took in some deep breaths, painfully pulling air into his lungs.

"What happened?" asked Saffin, offering a helping hand and guiding the other along the corridor towards the stairs.

For the time being, Cornelius was incapable of speech. Gesturing to his throat, he let himself be helped down the stairs. It was only when they reached the study that he managed to speak. "A violent spirit tried to strangle me. Fortunately, I don't think it was at full strength."

"You saw something? Tell me, what did it look like?" Walther eagerly demanded. "Was it all green and covered in pus, its head tucked under an arm with one eye hanging from its face as though it had just risen from the grave?"

"No." Despairingly, Cornelius shook his head, wondering for a moment just how this misguided American would react if he were to see the true horrors that existed on the other side.

Saffin, too, was finding their host's attitude annoying. "Mr. Walther, please try and understand that this is a very serious situation we have here. As I've told you, something terrible happened in this house and due to the fact that I've been having nightmares in which your son keeps trying to warn or inform me of an impending disaster, I think that—"

Walther rose from his chair. "Okay, okay. I get it! So what can we do about it? Should we move, is that what you're saying?"

"Moving won't resolve anything," said Cornelius emphatically, crossing his arms. For a man who had just survived being throttled by an unknown, invisible assailant he looked remarkably calm. "I think I know what's going on here and if I'm right we're all in danger."

"What kind of danger?" asked Mrs. Walther.

"Yes, just what is it you're getting at?" said Walther. It seemed only now that he was beginning to take things with the level of gravity they demanded.

"I think your son is either possessed or on the verge of being so and that the different powers within this house are vying for control of him. At the moment, he's completely unaware of this, at least his conscious mind is. However, he's been sending out signals in his sleep. Signals that Robert here has been receiving. It's as though Dominic has been making silent appeals for help."

"You're joking, right?" It seemed that Walther was all on for seeing Casper, or even the odd Halloween spook, but this was getting serious.

"This is not a frivolous matter," Cornelius retorted.

"Is there anything than can be done?" asked Mrs. Walther. "Should we contact a priest?"

"Call a priest and you'll never get your son back!" came a harsh, Geordie voice from the doorway.

All of them turned to see Dominic staring at them.

For a moment Cornelius saw the boy's face flicker as that of a rough-looking, unshaven man superimposed it. Then Dominic collapsed.

* * * *

Two hours later, Saffin, Cornelius and Dominic's parents were sat around a large circular table in the dining room, preparing to hold a séance. They had tried to get out but all of the doors were locked tight. None of the windows could be opened and they proved strangely unbreakable. The phone was dead. All indications were that Carrin-Bridge Manor and its non-human residents had no intention of letting them go.

Dominic himself had remained unconscious but his breathing remained regular and there was a healthy colour to his face. He lay slumped on a small bed his father had brought down from upstairs.

"Let us link hands and close our eyes. Don't open them or break the circle unless I tell you to. This is vitally important as I will first construct a mystical defence to protect us from outside attack." Cornelius closed his eyes, his face half-shadowed from the flickering light that came from the solitary candle in the middle. For the next five minutes he intoned and muttered strange words that none of the others had ever heard before.

Saffin sat with Cornelius on his right and Walther on his left. For a time there was nothing but silence and he found himself reflecting on just how unquestioningly he had come to accept all of these weird goings on. Once, not that long ago, he had been a respected Detective Inspector, one who, although open-minded, would never have embraced anything like this. However, he was different now. The nature of the deaths he had seen here and the dreams or visions or precognitions or whatever they were had made him re-evaluate all of his previous beliefs.

"I'd like to speak with whoever is inside Dominic," said Cornelius calmly, his eyes still shut. "Is it you, Jimmy Darlington or one of his gang?"

A cold sweat trickled down the side of Saffin's face. A slow creep of terror spread into his mind, threatened to pitch him into an abyss of madness and then dissipated once more as the protection from Cornelius' magic took force. However, this waiting, unseeing, was proving to be torture.

An agonising minute passed and still no response.

"I command you to come forth!"

A faint, chuckling laughter could be heard coming from the corner, from the bed in which Dominic lay. In his mind, Saffin pictured the child sitting upright, an evil smile on his face as he scornfully looked on the proceedings.

"I have the authority of the Inner Council to invoke the rite of exorcism." Cornelius' voice had changed. It was strident, authoritative. It was almost as though *he* had now become possessed by another being. "I will banish you to the Void if need be, where you will eat stones and drink dust for all eternity."

"Do that and the boy dies," snarled a man's voice from the shadow-filled corner.

Saffin had a sudden mental image of Darlington, or one of his thugs, holding the boy, a knife at his throat. After all, that was what it boiled down to. This was a psychic hostage situation.

"*No!*" Mrs. Walther screamed and sprang out of her chair followed a moment later by her husband.

Saffin felt the sudden drain as the defensive spell Cornelius had put in place fell apart. He heard screaming and, opening his eyes, he understood the reason for it. *The room was full of ghosts!* Five of them—the five suicides. The terrible apparition with half of his head blown away was standing directly behind Cornelius, a ghostly sawn-off shotgun in his hands. Next to Mrs. Walther was the man who had swallowed bag loads of dope and tipped dozens of pills down his mouth, his face a sickly yellow, his pupils huge and dilated. Reaching out for Walther was the drooling, blue-faced ghost of a man who had stuck his head in the gas oven. Grinning sadistically, sat on the bed by Dominic, was Darlington, a length of rope trailing from his neck to his right hand.

Saffin felt a tap on his shoulder and turned to see…

…the man was seated on the edge of a bed, shaking with fear. His face was white, his eyes bloodshot. He had the look of a man who had stared at his reflection and had seen something dreadful.

Saffin watched, unable to distance himself or interact with what was happening. It was as though he had become a mute, invisible spectator to the events that were unfolding. Incapable of helping himself, he followed as the man whom he knew was doomed, left the bedroom and began his way towards the bathroom at the end of the corridor.

Halfway there the two of them stopped as there came a loud bang, as of a shotgun going off, from one of the rooms further back.

The man hesitated for a moment, seemed to sag and then straightened himself. Entering the bathroom, he headed straight for the small cabinet above the sink, opened it and took out a packet of shaving razors.

Saffin gulped, knowing that he was going to be witness to this unfortunate's suicide.

Tearing open the packet with his teeth, the man then turned on the hot tap.

* * * *

"Wake up man! For God's sake, wake up!" shouted Cornelius.

Saffin screamed. He felt himself being roughly shaken. The nightmare vision was still in his eyes—blood squirting from a sliced wrist, circling away into the sink, turning the water a deep crimson. Next he felt a pair of strong arms locking under his, dragging him across the floor. "What…?" he began to mumble.

"Just take it easy." Cornelius helped the other into a chair. "You've been out for a while."

Saffin grasped his head. Some semblance of normality began to return and he could see that he was now in the lounge. A welcome fire was crackling in the hearth, providing light and warmth. Since primitive times man had known that these were two of the things that were needed in order to help dispel the darkness and the horrors that lurked within. It was just the two of them. There was no sign of any of the Walther family and thankfully no sign of the ghosts. "What happened and where are the others?"

"To answer your first question you've been locked in a spectral battle with one of the undead, as were we all. Luckily, I have some experience in combating these things and managed to shrug mine off fairly easily. I was then in a position to help you." Cornelius threw another log onto the fire. "I'm afraid the others have not been as fortunate."

"Are they…*dead?*"

"No, but neither are they alive," answered Cornelius, enigmatically. "At the moment I have them trapped within the dining room, though I can't say for how long. They've all succumbed to full possession. What is more, I fear that through my séance I may've inadvertently embodied them, permitting them to manifest outside their incorporeal selves."

"So what do we do? What *can* we do?"

"We've but one option. We must contact that which drove them to suicide in the first place. See if it will help us," answered Cornelius. He pulled up a chair.

"*What!?* It sounds insane. Surely whatever did that is more dangerous than Darlington and his gang." Clarity had now returned to Saffin's mind although part of him wished it hadn't. This situation, imprisoned within an old manor inhabited by a gang of vengeful wraiths was truly nightmarish.

"Maybe…but perhaps not as evil." Cornelius leant forward in his chair. "Think about it for a moment. This house has had no ghostly history for over a thousand years until those men set up their organisation here and start to conduct their criminal business. God knows what other nefarious things they got up to. You yourself have spoken of Darlington's cruelty and depravity. Could it not be that if some other force was here it would want them out?"

"So what are you saying? That maybe this place was haunted before by, shall we say, a good ghost and that it chose to dispose of Darlington and the others?"

"I'd say it's a possibility but we won't find out unless we reach out to it. Come to think about it, this could explain the telepathic communication you've been having with Dominic. Maybe this other spirit has been using Dominic to get in touch with you."

"Why?"

"Maybe it's trapped. Maybe it knows that it's outnumbered and needs the support that we can offer. Maybe it knew that by getting in touch with you, it would eventually get in touch with me." Cornelius grinned at his own reasoning, knowing that in reality there could be a thousand other reasons. If indeed he was on the right track at all. "What matters is that we need extra help and there's no one else at hand."

"All right. I'll follow your lead." Saffin was finding some of this confusing but right now Cornelius' idea of contacting this other entity seemed the only plausible one. It was either that or engage in a form of spectral brawl with the ghosts of five of the meanest, most violent Geordies he had ever had the misfortune of knowing. And in a scuffle of this nature he couldn't call for back-up or rely on the Newcastle upon Tyne Hospital Accident and Emergency department to patch him up afterwards. He could hear shouts and yells from the dining room. The door was repeatedly kicked and he heard a string of foul-mouthed expletives. It reminded him of the numerous weekend nights many years ago when he had driven the Black Maria, picking up the drunk and the disorderly. He dreaded to think what had become of the American family.

Cornelius nodded to himself and began his preparations, offering up sibilant prayers to whatever deity—or power—it was he believed in. He required no paraphernalia; no holy water or inscribed pentagrams. After five minutes or so, during which time the cries from the kitchen became increasingly vitriolic and nasty, he gestured to Saffin that he was ready.

Saffin drew his chair closer to the fire and sat opposite, watching as his companion fell into a trance. His lips were moving but otherwise *he* may as well have been dead.

As though the irate spirits knew something was happening they fell silent. Their silence more worrying than their roars of anger. For whilst they made their clamour Saffin knew where they were.

Something was moving around in the darkness and for a moment he felt the need to get up and switch the lights on, to flood the lounge with sane, bright electric light. He could hear a sound. The sound was not constant but built itself up from a low whimpering whisper to a dismal moan.

Then, with an alarming suddenness, an ethereal chalk-white face emerged from the shadows less than a foot away. It was as though it had just emerged through a gap in a dark velvet curtain. A hand appeared and then the phantom was pulling itself free, dragging its way out of some bizarre, inter-dimensional container.

"Fear ye not. My name is William Cavendish and I was once the owner of this place." The spirit was far less terrifying to behold than the others. It was that of an elderly man dressed in late Seventeenth Century attire as befitted a distinguished member of the landed gentry of that age. "As ye've no doubt guessed it was I who scared those ruffians who had dared to defile my property. No matter how hard I tried to persuade them to go, they would have none of it so I was forced to take drastic measures which I have since come to regret. How was I to know that my actions would result in their deaths or that they would return from beyond the grave in order to take revenge on me, forcing me to seek safety in a prison of my own making?"

"You mean you've been hiding from them?" Saffin asked, noticing with some relief that Cornelius was beginning to stir.

"I had no alternative. Remember there are five of them and I am, *was*, a man of peace."

"Yet you scared them enough that they took their own lives."

"As I said, this is something that I deeply regret," Cavendish said mournfully. "They left me with no alternative and I knew that by failing to act many more would die. In life I was a devout man, a man of God."

"Then why are you a ghost?" asked Cornelius. "Why haven't you passed over?"

"The Lord works in mysterious ways…maybe I remain here to ensure that the atrocity that has befallen this place is wiped away once and for all." Cavendish shrugged his shoulders. "Maybe I am here so that others may be saved."

"You mean Dominic and his parents?" asked Saffin.

The ghost merely smiled.

"So you'll help us?" said Cornelius.

Cavendish nodded. "I will help ye but I warn ye now it will be a hard-fought battle. The first thing we must do is utter a blessing in each of the rooms where those evil men killed themselves. By doing this we shall weaken them, hopefully to the point where we can make a direct attack. But we must hurry for I sense that the spell of binding ye've placed on the door is fading fast."

"Then let's go." Cornelius looked at Saffin who gave him a weary nod.

Following the apparition, the two men headed into the hall. Once there, Cavendish raised his spectral arms and the dangling corpse of Darlington appeared. Speaking in Latin, the ghostly clergyman began muttering a prayer of benediction.

The hanging corpse's eyes opened! "You've lost, priest. Victory is ours!" An evil, gargling laughter poured from its mouth. "We have the boy and his parents."

Saffin retreated in horror whilst Cavendish advanced, making the sign of the cross in the air, renewing his psychic battle. Cornelius joined in, uttering his own mystical phrases.

This two pronged attack took the spectre by surprise. It began to wither as a white glow surrounded Cavendish.

Thrashing like a fly in a spider's web, what remained of Darlington's hanging body began to decay. Everything speeded up so that he was now kicking and spinning at a mind boggling rate, becoming a blur, disintegrating. A moment later, he vanished, disappearing in an eye-watering cloud of foul-smelling vapour.

"Remember, this only weakens them. The spirit of that evil man is still in the dining room, still in the little boy." The ghostly reverend looked around, satisfying itself that the corpse-wraith was gone. "Now then, where next? Ah, the bathroom."

* * * *

It was as they were just finishing off in the upstairs bedroom, having dealt in the same manner with the suicide who had shot himself, that Saffin heard the dining room door below them smash open. He and Cornelius rushed out into the corridor to see Darlington and his undead cronies come charging up the stairs. As the paranormal investigator had feared, the revenants had now been given a semi-physicality, rendering them more zombie-like. The one with the sawn-off shotgun fired a round, the shot missing them by inches, blasting a hole in the wall.

The sight of those ghastly, anger-filled ghouls caused Saffin's heart to leap in his chest. He stumbled back into the room as with numerous violent cries they stormed inside.

Things then became a free-for-all; the ensuing punch-up like something from a surreal episode of *The Sweeney*.

Saffin found himself being attacked by the ghost with the slit-wrists and by the one that had taken the overdose. Both took a hold of him and, with a violent heave, flung him against a chest of drawers. He crashed against the piece of furniture, too surprised at the fact that they had been able to engage in physical violence to register the pain. Then things began hurting. He saw Cornelius laying into the horror with the blown away head, battering it to the ground before putting in some fierce kicks. Cavendish was in there as well, tussling with another. It looked as though he had already felled Darlington, for the latter was rolling about on the floor in agony.

A pair of icy hands gripped Saffin and hauled him to his feet. An ugly, grey-green, rotting face loomed in as he was butted and knocked to the floor once more. What he'd give for a group of the boys in blue to appear right now. They'd give this unruly lot of bastards what for and no mistake. With that thought, a memory of his time as a constable on the football terraces dealing with scores of rampaging hooligans came back, empowering him. He got to his feet, dodged a wild swing and waded in to the melee, fists flying, dealing out some good old fashioned police justice. Dragging one of the bruisers off Cornelius, he then flung him to one side. His hands felt slimy and he looked down to see they were dripping in glistening, ectoplasmic filth.

Had the ghoulish Geordie villains been at full strength there was no doubt that they would have put up more of a fight but as things were they had been psychically stripped of much of their vigour. Still, what they lacked in strength they made up for in increased numbers and brutish thuggery.

"Have a bit of this, you bastard!" Pulling a lout towards him by his scruffy tie, Saffin smacked him hard in the face with a clenched fist, the feeling not unlike punching cold porridge. Bits splattered.

Arms then locked around Saffin's back as he was effectively pinned. One of the ruffians hit him in the gut with a ring-studded ridge of knuckles. Instead of being hard and firm, the blow was wet and soggy, leaving an unsightly stain on his shirt. It still hurt though. Things were almost cartoonish in their brutality. He was hit a second time before Cornelius grabbed his attacker around the neck, putting him in a strangle-hold.

Elbowing the undead thug that held him, Saffin spun round and thumped him hard. A chair came flying from somewhere, narrowly missed his head and smashed against the wall. Then he was stumbling out into the corridor where he saw Cavendish wrestling on the floor at the head of the stairs. He raised an arm to fend off a slash from a knife, getting a deep gash for his troubles.

A figure charged out of the doorway. He met its rush, pivoted and tripped it up, its forward momentum carrying it on over the edge of the balcony. With a unearthly scream it landed in the hallway with a dull splash.

"Good work, Robert." Cornelius stepped out, panting and wiping his hands. His face and hair was covered in patches of unsightly ghost goo, but he appeared unharmed. He noticed Saffin's cut. "Are you all right?" he asked.

"It's just a scratch," Saffin answered. It was a bit more than that but it was nothing serious.

"Very good. Now to finish this."

The two of them rushed over to assist Cavendish but the benign spirit needed no such help. It stood up, the unmoving figure of Darlington at its feet. "Well, gentlemen. That seems to have taken care of those devils."

Saffin could hear some loud moans coming from inside the bedroom but he knew that they were the sounds of the incapacitated. There would be no more fighting from this lot. "What about the Walthers? Where are they?"

"If my guess is right, I'd say Dominic's inside him." Cornelius pointed down at Darlington. "His parents will be inside two of the others. Now that they've been beaten it shouldn't be that difficult a task to draw them out."

"Yes. Even now I can sense a certain level of tranquillity returning to Carrin-Bridge, one that has been missing for several years," said Cavendish. "Ye should find that the manor will no longer restrict ye from leaving. Once ye've successfully returned young Dominic and his parents I will see to it that these blaggards are permanently disposed of.

Never again will they be allowed to cause trouble here. May I thank ye both for helping me in ridding this place of their vile stain."

"I'm glad we could help," Cornelius replied. "Now then, I need to prepare myself for the ritual."

"Will the Walthers be all right, once you've freed them?" asked Saffin.

"Hopefully. There may be a trace memory buried deep within the spirit but nothing I should worry about. All being well it won't take too long before they forget about this whole damned experience."

* * * *

Dominic Walther sat on the edge of the window, staring down pensively at the people and the cars on the street far below. The memories and the bad dreams had come back and no amount of drugs or therapy would make them go away. He knew that something had happened to him when he had been a child during his family's brief stay in England—something bad—but what it had been his parents had never said. Both of them were dead now; his father having stuck his head in a gas oven, his mother having died from an overdose soon after.

Folk had said at the time that Simon Walther's suicide was attributable to stress at work; that of his wife's—grief at the loss of her husband, but he knew different.

Looking at the length of rope in his hand he also knew it was now time to join them, to *hopefully* rid himself of the nightmares once and for all.

THE FIDDLER IN THE FIRE

***Why had it laughed as all
around it burned?***

"Well, there are several different ways we can go about this, Miss Marston. Why don't you start by telling me a bit about your brother?" James Quinn reached for a pen and a pad of paper. Inwardly, he was excited, keen to be working on what he considered to be a proper case as opposed to the routine surveillance operations and petty fraud scams that had dominated his past two years.

Jacqueline Marston hesitated for a moment, unsure where to begin. Ever since her brother's disappearance she had found herself struggling to cope with even the most mundane of things. She took a deep breath. "Michael was…*is,* an unusual man, largely as a result of what happened to him twenty years ago. He was thirteen at the time." Removing a slim cigarette case from her handbag she took out a cigarette, lit it with a lighter and took a drag. "Did you ever hear about the Derry Funhouse tragedy?"

Quinn thought for a moment, dredging his memory. "It sounds vaguely familiar. There was a fire, wasn't there?"

"Yes…a terrible fire. The cause of which was never established although some suspicion was later levelled at my brother. Many children perished that day—or rather I should say *are presumed* to have perished, for their remains were never found, so severe was the fire. Michael was one of the two lucky ones…or so my parents thought at the time. For although he survived the inferno, he was never the same."

"I can well imagine there was some psychological scarring." Quinn could see that this was a case that would have to be handled delicately. It was hard to read the emotions on the woman's face. There was sorrow, but something else, something indefinable.

"Michael had terrible nightmares. I can still remember him screaming in the night as my parents desperately tried to console him. The doctors who were keeping a close eye on him became increasingly concerned and in the end it was recommended that he undergo professional psychiatric treatment. Bear in mind that he was still just a boy, his mind altered irrevocably by the horrors he had witnessed. As time went on he became increasingly disturbed, drawing strange pictures."

Jacqueline reached into her handbag for an envelope. She opened it and took out a folded piece of paper, which she handed over to the private investigator. "Here. Take a look.

Unfolding the paper, Quinn's eyes narrowed as he examined the drawings. All had been done with coloured pencils and whilst the uppermost two were but childish renderings of a flaming building, there was something unsettling about the ones beneath. These showed a leering, demonical being, wreathed in fire surrounded by burning stick-like figures. There appeared to be something resembling a violin in its hands and there was a savage, gleeful look in its eyes. It was almost as though whatever young Michael had depicted here was taking great delight in seeing these stick-people burn.

"Initially, he remained at home under my parents' and the doctors' supervision but as his mental condition deteriorated it was decided that he should be transferred to the Chester-Brooke mental hospital where he has spent virtually all of his adult life…up until two months ago."

Quinn had noted down the salient details. "And then what? Was he released or did he escape?" He regretted his choice of words a moment after he had asked the questions for it made it sound as though her missing brother was a prisoner, a criminal.

"He was released. The doctors had reached the decision that he wasn't a threat to society or himself and that there was little more that they could do for him. They thought that the best thing for him was to return to his family, try to get on and lead a normal life. As our parents are both dead now, it was agreed that he would come and live with me. For the first few weeks he was just like how I remembered him as a child. There didn't seem to be anything particularly wrong with him. However, as the days went by, he became more and more agitated, insisting that there was something that he had to do. When I asked him just what it was that was so important, he clammed up." Jacqueline stubbed out her cigarette. "Two days before he vanished I saw him sitting at the dining room table, drawing those fiendish pictures. I asked him what the pictures were supposed to represent. He looked at me and there was a look in his eyes…an intensity that I had never seen before. He pointed at his artwork and said in a voice I'll never forget: '*It* caused the fire. *It* played that hellish tune as all around it burned. *It* took their souls. I've got to destroy it.'"

Things were becoming strange. Quinn's brow wrinkled. "Forgive me, Miss Marston, but what exactly was your brother talking about? What is this '*it*' that he planned to destroy?"

Jacqueline hesitated, clearly uncertain how to proceed. And then, from the same envelope from which she had taken the drawings, she removed a newspaper cutting. It was yellowed with age. She handed it over. "This."

Quinn began to read the article.

Demolition teams working on the ruins of the old Derry Funhouse which was engulfed by fire on the 14th September 1953 resulting in the tragic deaths of thirty-seven children were surprised to uncover the relatively intact showpiece of the funhouse, 'Emperor Nero.' The thirty-year-old automaton which took pride of place within the main entrance is considered to be unique and its survival is most fortuitous considering that an initial report into the cause of the blaze suggests that it was here that the fire started. The Emperor is doubly lucky having been salvaged from Sunnyside Amusement Park nine years previously where an equally devastating fire occurred.

"I appreciate that this must all seem very unusual to you," Jacqueline admitted. "There is, however, a further piece of information which you may find interesting." She handed over another newspaper clipping.

Returning the first article to her, Quinn examined the second. Unlike the previous one, this one was dated to last year. There was a small photograph of a nervous-looking bespectacled man below which was:

Missing Person

Police are appealing to members of the public in the Churchville area to be on the lookout for missing thirty-one-year-old Jamie Watson. Jamie is five-feet seven inches tall, of medium build and has sandy coloured hair. Although friendly and considered to be no threat to the public, he is described as slightly delusional and has been on medication for psychological problems. If anyone has any information please contact the State Police.

"Jamie Watson was a friend of my brother. He was the other survivor of the fire. I managed to get in touch with his parents shortly after Michael went missing and they told me that he too had had extreme problems in dealing with what had happened and that he had been in and out of various psychiatric institutions. It was their belief that he had seen something other than just the fire, a view which was reinforced by his constant nightmares and from the things he would say. During the last few days before he disappeared, he became increasingly agitated, telling his parents that he had to go to Churchville and destroy *it* once and for all."

"Why Churchville? I fail to see the connection."

"I've been doing my own research in addition to rifling through some of Michael's old stuff, and it would appear that several years ago, an eccentric collector of amusement park memorabilia, a Mr. Edward Morose, bought 'Emperor Nero.' I tracked him down and he lives in a rundown mansion on the outskirts of the town."

"This is all very...*confusing*." There were numerous things about the details of this particular case that Quinn was finding hard to grasp. He was trying to logically think things through. From what he was hearing it seemed as though his client was implying that her brother and indeed the other unfortunate who had gone missing, believed that this funhouse attraction was in some way responsible for the conflagration that had claimed the lives of many of their school-friends. What was more, if he was reading her right, she, to some extent, shared this view. It was insane.

"I know this must all sound very strange to you but I'm begging you to help me find my brother. Whatever your price, I can pay it." There was a note of desperation now in Jacqueline's voice.

"Miss Marston." Quinn rested his elbows on his desk, bringing his palms together. "I take it that you've informed the local authorities of your brother's disappearance? I think it would be better if you were to report his last known movements to—"

"The police aren't interested," Jacqueline interrupted harshly, shaking her head. There was a bitterness to her tone. "As far as they're concerned my brother has just wandered off. They say that without any suspicion of foul play and taking into consideration what they refer to as my brother's 'psychological impairment,' this is what they term a 'mental health' issue, something out of their hands. Also, bear in mind that apart from advertising Jamie's disappearance in a newspaper they've done next to nothing in trying to locate *him*. And he's been missing for over a year.

"And I take it you believe that Michael went to Churchville, following in the footsteps of his friend?" If Quinn were to accept this case then at least he had somewhere to start his investigations, which was always a bonus.

"I know he did," answered Jacqueline emphatically.

"Well, it's all very intriguing, to say the least." Quinn had to admit that the background to this disappearance was unlike anything he had ever heard before. He didn't believe for one moment that there was anything unusual going on regarding the funhouse mannequin or whatever it was, reckoning that it was just a case of an extremely disturbed young man deciding to wandering off. Hopefully, all that would be required would be to spend a couple of days questioning the locals of Churchville as to whether or not they had seen him, maybe even paying this Edward Morose a visit. All things considered it shouldn't be that difficult and from the sounds of it the pay would be good.

Jacqueline's eyes lit up. "So you'll help? Will you come with me to Churchville to look for my brother?"

"Yes. I take it you want to begin as soon as possible? Would Monday be convenient?"

* * * *

"Martha!" The proprietor of the gas station, a scrawny old man in diesel-stained dungarees hollered to his wife who was in a back room. Chewing gum, he examined the somewhat grainy photograph a second time, shaking his head.

"He may have been here a week or so ago," added Quinn.

"I ain't seen him." The old man turned to the back room again. "*Martha!*" His shriek was painful on the ears, causing Jacqueline to wince.

An elderly lady in a wheelchair pushed her way into the doorway. Her face was wizened and there was a crotchety look about her. "What are you shoutin' about, Norm?"

Norm handed over the photograph. "You ever seen this man? These folk say he may have been in here. I told them I ain't ever seen him."

"Is he a crook?" Martha asked, staring fixedly at the photograph. "He looks like a crook. You can see it in his eyes." She was on the point of returning it to her husband when she suddenly stopped. "Hang on, I think I remember him. Young fella. Yeh, he came in here some days back. He was askin' directions. He went into the hardware shop next door and bought somethin.' I remember Ralph mentionin' it, thinkin' it damned peculiar. Now what was it?"

"Please, can you tell us where he wanted to go?" asked Jacqueline excitedly.

Martha shook her head. "My memory ain't as good as it used to be I'm afraid. I'm eighty-five, you know. Ralph would probably remember but he's goin' to be out o' town for the next week or so."

"Please, think." Jacqueline was imploring her now. "It's vitally important."

The old woman was clearly wracking her brains, her right hand shaking noticeably with the mental strain. She pulled at her bottom lip. "It may have been the Morose place, but I'm not entirely sure. Why he'd want to go up there God only knows."

"Thank you, you've been of immense help," Jacqueline said.

Quinn gave her a knowing nod. As leads went this was as good as any. The Morose place was always going to be one of the main points of call but to have it confirmed as such in this manner was most welcome. Together, they turned and prepared to leave.

"I just remembered what it was that the man bought. I knew it would come to me," Martha called out, catching them at the door. "A chainsaw."

* * * *

"I can't say that I like it." Jacqueline shivered, trying to keep the horror and revulsion out of her voice. She was certain that she must have seen it before, having been in the Derry

Funhouse as a child prior to that fateful day twenty years ago but she hadn't paid it any real attention.

"Oh, it's just a clockwork dummy," Quinn told her reassuringly. Yet, truth be told, he wasn't all that keen on it either. It was life-size, sat on a throne and contained within a thick glass cabinet, on the outside of which was an intricate metal box into which money could be inserted to make it move. The wax face was tilted back, mouth-open, frozen in mid-laugh. There was an undeniable grotesqueness to it which was most unnerving and the tufts of black hair that protruded from the sides of its head and grew from under the laurel wreath and crown it had rakishly perched on its head all leant a certain macabre, sinister quality to it. It wore thick, velvet robes. In its human-like hands it held a fiddle and a fiddlestick. He had seen something like this once at a fairground on Coney Island. For a nickel that one had told fortunes. If this one did the same he dreaded to know what terrible predictions it would make.

The smartly dressed, elderly, white-haired owner of the weird house they now found themselves in; a man who claimed to be of Irish descent and who had introduced himself as Edward Morose, gave a knowing smile. "He's far more than a mere dummy, let me assure you." He lovingly stroked the outside of the protective case. "He *is* the Emperor Nero. He was in a very sorry state when I...*procured* him. You wouldn't believe the amount of work that I've had to do in order to return him to something of his former glory."

The three of them were stood on the wide, double landing in the impressive hallway.

"Where did you get it?" Quinn asked conversationally. Like the dummy, there was something about Morose that he didn't quite like, something *unsettling,* particularly in the way he kept looking at Jacqueline. They had come here on the pretext that they had broken down just a bit further up the road. A cunning plan that he hoped would enable them to have a good snoop around without arousing any unwarranted suspicion on the part of the other. There was no denying the fact that Morose was weird; some of the things he had already shown them amongst his bizarre collection of largely fairground and freak-show exotica had bordered on the truly ghastly. The question was whether he was involved in any way with Michael's disappearance.

"Ah, now there's a story," replied Morose. "Let's just say that it wasn't easy. In fact, I'd even go as far as to say that of all my acquisitions he was without doubt the hardest." He eyed Jacqueline hungrily, smiling as he noticed the displeasure on her face. He looked at Quinn. "But I can see that your good lady is not that taken by him. Perhaps now's the time to retire for a drink and a bite to eat. If you'd just follow me I'll see if my butlers have prepared something for us." He turned and headed back down the stairs.

"You have more than one butler?" asked Jacqueline.

"In a manner of speaking, yes," answered Morose guardedly.

Jacqueline had already averted her gaze from the dummy in the cabinet but Quinn wasn't finding it easy to do so. It was almost as though its glassy, doll-like eyes were watching him. Was it just his imagination or were there tiny flames burning deep within the blackness of its pupils?

Quinn gulped and managed to divert his gaze, thankful that its owner had not insisted on activating it—assuming that it worked. The last thing he wanted to see right now was that inanimate being stir into action, for it to start rocking on its throne, fiddling away and emitting spine-tingling guffaws of laughter. He shuddered at the thought.

"As I told you, I'm afraid the storm appears to have damaged the telephone line, not that you'd be able to get a mechanic to come out here at night anyway," claimed Morose as he lead his two guests towards the dining room. "I don't often get visitors stuck away out here so please forgive me if my social skills aren't what they should be." He gestured for them to enter.

Like the rest of the main rooms on the ground floor they had already been shown, the dining room was spacious but something of a throwback to an earlier age. The lighting was very dim and came from several kerosene lamps which cast unsettling shadows across the long table complete with its frayed lace covering, trays, plates, cutlery, napkins and silver cloche. Two dust-covered wine bottles and several glasses rested nearby. Creepy-looking portraits hung on the walls. What other furniture they could see looked old and battered. Cobwebs clung to the pair of candlesticks on the mantelpiece. A tattered, moth-eaten curtain screened the large French windows. There was a strong, somewhat off-putting smell in the room. It was as though a dead cat lay festering under the floorboards.

Morose took his place at the head of the table whilst the other two sat at the opposite end.

"I'd like to thank you once again for being so…hospitable, Mr. Morose," said Quinn insincerely. He glanced down at the bowl of steaming brown-green liquid with some level of disgust and wariness. It looked most unpalatable.

"Yes." Jacqueline nodded in agreement but she too was feeling very uncomfortable with things. Maybe this wasn't such a good idea after all.

"The soup is from an old Irish recipe," said Morose. He started to take several spoonfuls.

Warily, his two guests did the same, both pleasantly pleased to discover that the soup was surprisingly nice, if a little peppery.

"So who else stays here aside from yourself and your… butlers?" asked Quinn, having to peer across the table at his host such was the dimness. Since their arrival just over an hour ago they had not seen anybody else. A place as big as this surely necessitated the presence of some domestic staff, although it was clear that the master of the house didn't employ any cleaners.

"No one." Morose put his spoon down. "I daresay there are certain household chores that I've neglected over the years and there's much work that could be done to the grounds but on the whole I'm quite satisfied with how things are. Yes, I could employ someone to assist me with the collection and indeed I did for a while…" He paused for a moment before changing the subject. Rising to his feet, he paced to the centre of the table, lifting the lid off the cloche to reveal the succulent, bloody roast underneath. "Well, now that you seem to be coming to the end of your soup may I tempt you with a little beef?" He reached for a large knife and began carving, unceremoniously dropping the sliced slivers onto plates.

"It's almost raw," Jacqueline mouthed distastefully to Quinn whose heart sank and whose gorge rose as he watched the blood pool out from the beef and leak across the plates. He knew people who liked their steaks rare but he preferred his meat well-cooked, blackened almost.

Morose looked up. "How much can you eat? Three slices? Four?" He resumed his cutting.

Quinn couldn't help but notice the pleasure with which Morose drew the sharp blade through the dead flesh. His host was clearly enjoying what he was doing and there was something rather troubling in that. "To be honest with you, Mr. Morose, I don't think I'm all that hungry. I had something at a diner not that long ago—"

"Nonsense," Morose interrupted, dismissively waving the hand that held the knife. "A man like you needs his meat. It's a good source of protein, you know." He handed over a plate with three bloody cuts on it before looking at the woman. "And what about you, my dear? Same again?"

"Sorry, no. I'm afraid I'm a strict vegetarian." Jacqueline smiled, hoping her inspired lie would suffice in deterring the other.

"A vegetarian? Oh dear." Morose shook his head disapprovingly. "Ah, well, I suppose someone has to be. I guess I'd better not tell you what was in the soup." Choosing not to elaborate, he instead reached for one of the age-old wine bottles. "I've had this bottle in my cellar for as long as I can remember. I've been saving it for a very special occasion. Maybe there will be cause to open it later tonight?" He put it back down and reached for the other bottle.

"I'm afraid neither of us drink," said Quinn. Right now he needed a strong bourbon but there was no way he was going to partake of anything out of those bottles. Besides, he detested wine.

Jacqueline nodded, colluding in his deceit.

"How peculiar." Reluctantly, Morose returned the bottle to the table. "Well, once we've had our main course maybe we can retire to the study."

Quinn stared for a moment at his unpalatable meal. It was just cuts of meat, swimming in a puddle of blood. There were no vegetables. He was finding it hard to accept that it was beef, thinking somewhat sickeningly that perhaps Morose had murdered Michael and was now serving him up. He almost retched at the thought.

"Maybe it would be best if we started walking to Churchville," said Jacqueline.

"Not at all. Churchville's a good ten miles from here and in the dark it would be so easy to lose your way. Besides, as I told you, I'm expecting a delivery early tomorrow morning and when the driver arrives you can take a ride with him. I've also got a feeling in my bones that there's a storm brewing. You'd get soaked and I wouldn't want the prospect of you both coming down with hypothermia on my conscience, now would I?"

Morose picked up his plate and went back to his chair. He sat down and began on his meat. He was a messy eater, chewing noisily. Blood drooled from the corner of his mouth, dripped from his chin and stained his smart white shirt making him look like a vampire. With a muffled apology he dabbed at the leakage with a napkin.

There came a strangled moan from beyond the door.

"If you'll excuse me a moment." Morose got to his feet.

Quinn sat watching as the door creaked open and although he could not tell who it was that was beyond, for some reason a shiver of revulsion passed through him.

Morose stepped through and closed the door behind him, leaving the two of them alone for the time being.

"I want to get out of here," whispered Jacqueline.

"I know what you mean but it's important that we stay in order to find out more. I'm sure that something very strange is going on here." Quinn looked around, trying to take in the shadowy details, hurriedly using the opportunity of their host's absence to toss his untouched meat into an unlit corner. "I honestly think that there's a lot more to be discovered. I'll admit he's weird and that there's something most disturbing about that thing in the cabinet, but—"

The door opened suddenly and Morose returned, clapping his hands. "Ah, I see you've finished. I hope the meal proved satisfactory. Now, I think it would be for the best if we retire to the study, that is unless you wish to have an early night. It's already quite late and I daresay you've been travelling long. My butlers have just informed me that your rooms are prepared, so I'll leave it to you to decide."

Quinn thought for a moment, trying to reach a decision. He was sorely tempted to ask his host whether or not he had seen Michael. From past experience, he had learned that sometimes the direct approach was the best. He had his suspicions; wondering whether or not this strange man had played some part in Jacqueline's brother's disappearance. For the time being, he decided to maintain his subterfuge in the knowledge that by doing so he might discover more than asking the man outright. He turned to the woman. "Well, what do you think?"

Jacqueline shrugged her shoulders. "It's up to you. I am tired," she said, keeping her options open.

"Well, that being the case, I'll show you to your rooms." Morose led them out of the dining room.

* * * *

The bedroom was incredibly dusty, with large cobwebs hanging from the defunct chandelier. The carpet was stained and threadbare and that terrible smell Quinn had detected in the dining room lingered in the air. A disturbing portrait of an elderly woman in an old-fashioned black shawl stared out at him from the shadows and one of the first things he had done had been to check that there were no secret spy-holes in the wall behind it.

It was now half-past midnight and Quinn had absolutely no intention of going to sleep. He sat in a large padded chair in one corner of the room, a small desk-lamp on, idly leafing through a rather battered version of Mary Shelley's *Frankenstein*, waiting for a suitable time to begin a search of the house in the hope that he might discover something relating to Michael's disappearance.

Placing the book down on a small table, Quinn got to his feet, switched on his small torch and went over to the door. He stopped, listening to every little sound, his nerves stretched taut. Satisfied that he could hear nothing, he quietly opened the door and stepped out into the carpeted corridor.

He had pre-arranged to rendezvous with Jacqueline sometime after midnight, and as he crept towards her door at the far end, he went over what he planned to say if, in the process of their search, they encountered the owner of the house or one of his butlers. He would explain that he suffered from somnambulism and that Jacqueline followed him to ensure that he did not harm himself by falling down the stairs or leaving the house and that she was taking him back to his room.

The door to Jacqueline's room was locked.

Quinn tried the handle. Nothing. He rapped as loudly as he dared, hoping to get her attention. There was no answer. Bewildered, he stepped away from the door, surreptitiously looking around for any signs of movement, half-expecting to see Jacqueline coming along the corridor towards him, in the belief that she had lost patience in him and had decided to instigate her own investigations. For a brief moment he was aware of something, something dark and unseen, skulking at the far end of the corridor. He strained his eyes in order to make it out but it refused to come into focus, to yield a definite outline so that he might recognise it.

He stood there, numbly trying to control the strange thrill of fear in his mind. The muscles of his stomach corded, and were pulled tight by a sense of rising anxiety. Why was the door locked and more importantly why was there no reply to his knocking? And what had been that thing at the end of the corridor?

Damn it all, he thought angrily, mustering his courage. If Morose was up to any tricks then he would soon be regretting them. Clenching his right fist, he stalked purposefully along the corridor, ready and more than willing to strike the first thing that emerged from the shadows.

In the light from his torch, Quinn stared about him. He reached the place where he had sensed something moving, and, noting that the room door facing him was slightly ajar, he pushed it open. Like several of the other rooms he had seen when Morose had led both he and Jacqueline upstairs, this one was crammed full of weird oddities, more of the stuff that was on display in the rooms downstairs. Dozens of marionettes and puppets of every description, horrid little things, hung in twisted poses from the ceiling creating ghastly shadows on the floor and the walls.

There was nobody in there. At least nobody that he could see. With a gulp, Quinn closed the door. Outside, a branch tapped softly on the pane of a window and a shadow slid noiselessly across the floor. In spite of the tight hold he had on himself, fear was mounting swiftly inside, clawing at his brain.

He was now on a long gallery, its wood-panelled walls decorated with tattered fairground posters and flyers advertising magic acts. Looking over the banister, he could see below him the shadowy outline of the glass case in which that awful automaton resided. Edging forward, he was just about to start downstairs when he heard a door opening behind him.

Turning, Quinn's heart skipped a beat as he saw two ghastly Oriental faces grinning at him in the torchlight not ten feet away. They were so close to one another that at first he thought it was one man looking over the other's shoulder but he was stunned almost to the point of paralysis when he saw that *both heads were attached to the same body*! There was an uncanny surrealism to this and he now understood why Morose had spoken of his 'butlers' in the plural—for they were a frightfully ugly pair of Siamese twins, conjoined from the necks down, with two arms and two legs. The light glinted from the knives held in each of their hands.

"Jesus Christ!" Panic and terror threatened to overwhelm Quinn. On legs that felt as though they had turned to jelly, he stumbled down the stairs, narrowly avoiding a trip. He rushed past the 'Emperor Nero' and bounded down the last few remaining steps, skidding to a halt in the tiled, main hall.

Despite their deformity, the twins moved quickly, casting a bizarre shadow, their actions spider-like. Loping on their long and spindly legs, they sprang in pursuit, leaping down the stairs, a maniacal, murderous look on their horrible faces.

Suddenly the whole room lit up as the lights went on.

Quinn blinked and shielded his eyes from the stabbing illumination. The door to the study opened and, with a scream, Morose came charging at him, a heavy-looking silver candlestick in his hand. Before Quinn could protect himself the other had struck out, bringing it down heavily on his head.

* * * *

Moaning in the darkness, Quinn painfully regained consciousness. He lay sprawled on a cold, damp floor.

"Are you all right?"

Quinn turned on hearing the voice which had come from over on his left. The darkness was pervasive and he couldn't see anything.

"Can you hear me?"

Groggily, Quinn got to his feet, massaging his head. There was one hell of a bump there. He staggered to one side, supporting himself against a wall with an outstretched hand. "I can hear you. Who are you and where are we?"

"My name's Michael Marston, and right now you're in the basement of the Morose mansion."

"*Michael!* Thank God you're alive!" Quinn edged his way forward, coming up short against a wall of metal bars. He was in a cell of some sort. "My name's James Quinn and I've come here with your sister, Jacqueline, to find you."

"Jacqueline's here!?" There was a note of heightened concern in Michael's voice. "Where is she? Is she with you?"

"No. I ran into some weird twins and then Morose cracked me on the skull. Next thing I know I'm in here. Have you any idea what's going on?"

"Only too well I'm afraid." There was something in the way that Michael answered Quinn's question that he didn't like. "I don't know how much Jacqueline has told you, but it's all to do with…the Emperor Nero. The thing he has in the glass case. You see, I know Morose's and it's secret. I know everything about it. I was there. I saw it laughing and fiddling as all around it burned. And I also know that Jacqueline's in grave danger."

"What can you tell me about it?" Quinn asked, blindly trying to locate the lock on the cage he was trapped in. He was quite handy with a lock-pick and he had been doubly fortunate in that he had one in his back pocket and his captors had not confiscated it. Throughout his career as a private investigator he had had recourse to use it on numerous occasions to open locked doors and filing cabinets. However, this was the first time it would be used to break out of somewhere.

"Morose, the man you see, is not really a man," Michael explained. "He's but an extension, the outward projection of the thing that lives inside Emperor Nero, a thing that is pure evil. I don't know whether it's a demon or what, but it feeds on death and destruction and it uses Morose to ensure that it's supplied with victims. Twenty years ago, it was Morose, in the guise of a janitor, who locked all the doors of the fun-house which he subsequently set ablaze. Fortunately, a friend of mine, Jamie Watson, knew a secret way in, through which we managed to escape. However, that's all insignificant. What really matters is that I believe there's something truly fiendish in store for Jacqueline. Although it's limited in power, in the sense that it can only exert its will through Morose, one of the ways that this entity can escape its confines is through an unholy marriage. Oh God! I never thought she'd follow me here," he said despairingly.

Quinn couldn't bring himself to believe any of this. It was all nonsense, it had to be. The product of an undoubtedly sick and deeply troubled mind. Yes, Morose was an abducting psychopath who as soon as he got out of here was going to be in serious trouble, along with his two-headed freak of a butler but, as to being what Michael described…

He found the lock and began to pick it, his task impeded by the darkness.

"It's no use trying to force these locks. I've tried countless times and—" Michael stopped upon hearing the other's cell door swing open. Shuffling movement indicated that Quinn was edging his way around the confines of the room, searching for something.

A moment later, an overhead strip light lit the cluttered basement in a harsh, actinic glare.

"Right, let's get you out of there." Quinn went over to Michael's cage, seeing for the first time the haggard and half-starved look on the young man. "How long have you been in here and how have you survived?" he asked.

"I've lost track. Four or five days. A week. Kang and Kung, the Siamese twins, occasionally bring down water and food. As to why I'm being kept alive, I don't truly know. I've given this some thought and the only thing I can think of is that it's as a precautionary measure in case anything happens to Morose's physical body. The demon, if that's what it is, could then take mine. If my theory is right, then you're still alive for the exact same reason. In fact, as you're in much better condition than me they'll probably kill me and keep you as the spare instead."

That there was madness here Quinn was certain, but right now he had heard enough. Skilfully, he unlocked the cage door. "Time to get out of here and find your sister." He looked about, searching for anything that could be used as a weapon. He didn't think that Morose could put up much of a fight but there was always the odd twins. Spotting an iron crowbar resting atop a stack of crates in one corner, he went over and picked it up, giving it a few swings.

"Nothing short of full dismemberment of Nero will bring an end to this horror," said Michael. He started rummaging frantically among the stacked crates. "I think they threw it in here after they caught me." Dragging aside a sheet of tarpaulin he uncovered a stout chest. Crouching down, he heaved it open, reached inside and withdrew a chainsaw. "Good. Now let's finish this and see about rescuing my sister."

Determinedly, the two of them climbed the flight of wooden stairs that led out of the basement. At the top was a door which they opened, finding themselves in a dark and shadowy parlour. Faint fairground music came from somewhere nearby as though someone were playing a calliope. There was an unsettling, haunting, almost evil sound to the weird melody that was being played.

"Can you hear that?" asked Michael.

Quinn nodded although he wished that he couldn't hear it. There was something deeply disturbing about it that sent a shiver straight through him. Why was it that something commonly associated with fun and pleasure conjured up so many darkly mysterious and frightening images—prancing, sinister-faced clowns in their garish costumes and make-up; villainous, grinning ringmasters overly keen to welcome the little children into the circus and sideshow freaks of all shapes and sizes emerging from the shadows? His grip on the crowbar tightened, his knuckles white.

Michael crept up to the door that led to the hallway and pushed it slightly, peeking beyond.

It seemed to Quinn that Michael had frozen; that he was in shock at what he was witness to. "What is it? Tell me." When the other failed to answer, he pushed him out of the way in order to see for himself and for a moment swirling insanity threatened to tear his mind apart.

Long, sable banners had been draped over the banisters of the double flight of stairs and tall candelabras, filled with flaming candles, illuminated the hallway in an infernal glow. Everything had been terrifyingly transformed, decorated with the more macabre of Morose's strange collection which were warped and lengthened by a series of funhouse mirrors, creating dimensionally confusing phantasmal reflections. Blackened, twisted, half-formed things lurked within the curved, polished glass panels; trapped but eager to escape.

At the base of the stairs, cranking an old-fashioned hand-organ, were the Siamese twins, dressed in a strangely tailored morning dress. They were clearly providing the musical accompaniment to the ceremony which was taking place on the landing—*the bizarre marriage of Jacqueline Marston to the thing in the glass cabinet!*

Somehow, Quinn managed to retain a grip on his senses. He could see Morose presiding over the events as though he were a priest, mouthing strange words that he couldn't understand, offering his unholy blessings. Jacqueline appeared to be immobile, whether drugged or bewitched he didn't know.

Now free from its cabinet, the thing that had gone by the name of Emperor Nero stood tall and proud.

For a moment, it felt to Quinn as though his mental capabilities had turned to sludge. It seemed as though something within his mind hadn't snapped as such, but rather had become gelatinous, slipping away like a damp rag, his thoughts and perceptions inchoate. Unsteadily, he staggered against the door, temporarily unable to take in and come to terms with what his eyes were showing him. Madness would have taken him completely had it not been for the sudden loud sound of Michael starting up the chainsaw not two feet from where he stood, the noise jarring him back into some form of reality—a reality in which a demonic automaton that was responsible for the deaths of many children was now entering into nuptial bliss with the man with the chainsaw's sister.

"I'm going to get you, you bastard!" screamed Michael, rushing forward, buzzing chainsaw held aloft.

Quinn charged in behind him, rushing for Kang and Kung, aware that the grotesque horrors in the mirrors—the perverse wedding guests—had seen him and were desperately trying to claw their way out of their dimensional prisons. The Siamese twins were quick, drawing their knives and kicking the music-machine over, hatred burning in their four eyes. Quinn dodged the blades and brought the crowbar down on one of the ugly heads, knocking his foes to the ground. Frantically, he continued to beat, deaf to the others' pleas, reducing both heads to bloody pulps. He looked up to see how Michael was doing, noticing that Morose had been cut down and now lay at the base of the steps, dark purple ichor pooling out from beneath him.

Michael was locked in fierce combat with the ghastly automaton, wrestling for possession of the chainsaw whilst Jacqueline, free from her trance, had retreated to the top of the stairs, a horrified look on her face.

It was at times like this that Quinn regretted not having a gun. Although whether that would have proved of any use against this unearthly creature he didn't know. He was no coward, and, gripping the blood-dripping crowbar, he determinedly ran up the stairs in order to join the melee. He had only gone half a dozen steps when he saw Michael being forcibly pushed back against the waist-high banister. And then, he was thrown over it, landing with a sickening thud on the tiled hallway floor some ten feet below, the chainsaw skidding from his hand.

Lambent fires of pure malice burned in the Emperor Nero's black, raven-like eyes as it began down the stairs towards Quinn, its arms extended, fingers spread as if it wanted to throttle the life from him.

Quinn hurled the crowbar at it, cursing as the thing sidestepped and the heavy tool flew over its shoulder. Then it came at him, bounding down the last of the steps, smacking him with a vicious backhand that sent him reeling. Before he could fully get to his feet it grabbed him, spinning him effortlessly across the hallway, smashing him face first against a wall. It felt as though he had been kissed by a reversing pickup truck. Spitting out a tooth, he crumpled to the floor, blood streaming from his mashed nose and mouth.

A menacing shadow fell around his battered body.

Viciously, Quinn was lifted, raised off the ground, his back to the wall, powerful hands at his throat. He saw himself mirrored in the twin black orbs of the thing's eyes. Its mouth was wide open; a dark drain from which obscene gargling noises came like sewage pouring down a pipe. And then there was laughter; bloodcurdling, nightmarish guffaws that heralded the end of the private investigator. His mind was darkening.

"*Die!*" With a savage cry, Jacqueline plunged the chainsaw straight through the thing's back. Dislodging a heap of ghastly innards, the buzzing, bladed saw emerged through the thing's front, coming to a stop less than an inch from Quinn's groin. She then withdrew it and brought it down, sawing into the Emperor Nero's left collarbone.

Sprayed with purple, demonic blood, Quinn was dropped. Rubbing his bruised neck, he watched, helplessly, as Jacqueline gruesomely severed one arm from the thing before setting about carving at the other arm. Michael had survived the fall and was nearby, shouting at her, instructing her to cut it into pieces.

Painfully, Quinn got to his feet. Everything ached. Through unbelieving eyes, he watched as Jacqueline removed the head and the legs.

Soon it was over, the dismemberment complete.

Quinn went to put an arm around Jacqueline and it was then that he saw a sudden flash of movement. The dreadful mirror-wraiths were burning, their actions frantic. It was as though whatever they were, they were experiencing a terrible death beyond death.

"Oh my God!" Still gripping the chainsaw, Jacqueline pointed down at the Emperor Nero's scattered remains. Glistening, purple appendages sprouted from the stumps and were attaching themselves to the removed limbs and head, drawing them back onto the body.

The three of them withdrew in utter horror.

"Michael!" an unearthly voice wailed from one of the mirrors.

All of them turned in that direction, but it was only Michael who identified his friend, Jamie Watson, his features strained as though he was exerting all of his energy in battling to present his true image.

"You must smash the mirrors. Free us!"

As though the demon within the automaton had understood what the mirror-wraith had said, it moved to try and position itself, to protect the reflective panels.

It couldn't stop all three of them, moving to block Quinn as the other two launched themselves forward, picking up anything they could use in order to start breaking the funhouse mirrors in which whatever these things were that were inside had been contained.

In an act of desperation, the reconstituted Emperor Nero hurled Quinn forward. The private investigator stumbled and crashed against one of mirrors. The glass splintered and cracked and suddenly he felt a hand reaching out from within. For a moment, he felt as though something was going to pull him in and that he too would be forever damned and imprisoned in the nightmarish dimension beyond but he found himself pushed aside instead.

And then there were children screaming and streaming out from all directions, infants and adolescents, vengeful victims of this unholy being. The hallway became packed as with a mad frenzy they set upon the demon, doing unto it what Jacqueline had been unable to do with the chainsaw, tearing it into much smaller pieces, trampling it underfoot and destroying it utterly before fading away.

Jacqueline threw her arms around her brother. She was sobbing.

Sitting down on one of the steps, Quinn surveyed the wrecked hallway, unable to fully come to terms with all that had transpired. His mind turned to the rooms and rooms of macabre marionettes and puppets and for one horrible moment he had a vision of each of them becoming host to that which had inhabited the Emperor Nero. "Michael!" he called out. "There were cans of kerosene in the basement, weren't there?"

"Yeah, I think so."

Tiredly, Quinn got to his feet. "Come on, we've got one last job to do. Soon we'll be the only ones laughing as this place burns to the ground."

THE MAN IN CABIN D166

*Was he the reason why no one was
ever found aboard the Athena?*

"In my professional opinion, what you need, more than anything, is a long vacation. Have you ever considered going on a cruise?"

John Warner had never cruised before—hell, he couldn't remember the last holiday he'd been on. It must've been ten years ago at least, back when Beth, his wife, had been alive. He tensed slightly, closing his eyes as a momentary shadow passed over his heart and the old, soul-aching memory of her face flickered across his mind. So young to die…so beautiful. Why could God be so cruel as to keep him alive without her? It was a question he had asked himself a thousand times. He found himself gulping back the tears.

"Are you all right, Mr. Warner?" Doctor Edwards, a young consultant, fixed his patient with a concerned look.

Warner massaged his brow. "Yes, it was just a…realisation, I guess, that I haven't been on holiday for quite some time."

"Well, now that your compensation case is finally over, and you're now a very wealthy man, as your treating clinician, I strongly advise that you take some time out. Get away from it all for a month or two. I've been quite meticulous in going through your previous neuropsychologist, Doctor Carpenter's, notes and, as you've been informed, the head injury you sustained in the car accident *will* have lifelong effects.

However, that said, your response to your therapy sessions has been phenomenal."

Warner nodded. "So I've been told. My memory is nowhere near as good as it should be and as you know my speech is sometimes a bit slurred. Occasionally I have rather disturbing thoughts, and the flashbacks still come and go."

"It's now almost seven years post-accident and I'd like to assure you that everything you've experienced and described—all of the symptoms—are classic indicators of mild organic personality disorder resulting from a severe closed head injury. All of your past emotive, morbid thoughts and paranoid delusions are perfectly 'normal' given the damage inflicted on your brain." Doctor Edwards briefly consulted the medical papers in front of him. "I'm pleased to note that there have been marked improvements in your cognitive abilities."

Warner shrugged noncommittally. He had lost count of how many 'monkey-tests,' as he thought of them, he had been subjected to over the past many years; all of them undertaken in order to establish the severity of his injury. It had soon become apparent that the damage was not specifically in relation to his intelligence but rather to his personality. He had suffered from waves of intense anger and crippling despair and had turned to drink, becoming a borderline alcoholic; anything to provide some level of escapism. Indeed, he would be hard pushed to remember the last time he had gone to bed sober. Prior to his accident he had been a teetotaller.

"I'll say it again, what you need is a—"

"A vacation," Warner interrupted. "Yes…but a cruise? Do you really think it would be a good idea?" In spite of his doubt, he was inwardly excited at the prospect.

Doctor Edwards nodded enthusiastically. "I'm absolutely certain. In fact, I gave the very same recommendation to one of my other patients whose problems were very similar to your own. On his return he was like a new man. Maybe not his old self but his levels of optimism and his self-confidence had improved dramatically, and seemingly permanently, upon his return. Believe me, what you need right now is a break. You've been carrying this burden for so long now that you've forgotten how to enjoy yourself."

Warner sat for a moment, deep in thought, mulling things over. There was no denying the fact that the past seven years had been, by and large, filled with despondency, unbearable grief, rage and misery. Following the accident he had been in a coma for three months, mercifully unaware that his wife was dead and that his career as a research scientist was now effectively over. Upon regaining consciousness, and after having being told the tragic news, he had only hoped for one of two things—death, or for the doctors to put him back into blissful sleep.

Somehow, after years of brain scans, consultations and therapy, in addition to having to endure six and a half years of an exceedingly painful and protracted litigation against the driver of the truck who had jumped the lights and had caused the crash, he had survived.

And now he was offered a chance—a chance to try and turn his life around, to salvage something from the wreckage of his past. He was realistic enough to know that going on a cruise wasn't going to miraculously repair the damage caused to his frontal lobes or bring his wife back, but it might just act as a catalyst to kick-start the long road to a happier existence. He had been constantly reminded that, in one way, he ought to be thankful for the fact that he was alive and that the damage sustained had not completely incapacitated him. Yes, he was psychologically impaired and would forever remain so but, at thirty-seven, he still had a lot of life to look forward to. Surely now it was time to move on.

He was still ruminating when he saw Doctor Edwards reach into a drawer and slide over a glossy magazine.

* * * *

Upon leaving the hospital, Warner went straight to the only travel agency in the Main Street, the cruise brochure under one arm. He whistled jauntily to himself, feeling more upbeat and optimistic than he had for a long time, having decided that he would take his doctor's advice.

Once inside the travel agency he was bombarded with a confusing barrage of information—there were numerous cruises he could choose from all of varying durations and itineraries.

"Was there anything particular you were interested in, sir?" inquired the bespectacled young woman behind the desk.

For a moment Warner was confused, unable to comprehend the fact that he was even here. Prior to this moment, his life since the accident had revolved around a routine drudgery wherein everything was more or less the same. Due to the nature of his head injury, one of his main problems had been social interaction with people he did not know. He felt both embarrassed and frustrated, momentarily uncertain how to answer her question. Numbly, he opened the travel brochure Doctor Edwards had given him prior to leaving his clinic.

"We currently have some special deals on our New England and Canadian voyages. It's an ideal time of year to travel. No schoolchildren and the weather should be very pleasant." The woman smiled cheerily.

"I've been told that cruise X390 is the one for me." Warner handed over the magazine. On the open page were all of the necessary details pertaining to the voyage in question, in addition to a spectacular photograph of the ship.

"*Cruise X390?* Why, that's one of our most exclusive packages." She stared at him, obviously considering whether or not he would be able to afford the cost. There was nothing blatant about him that struck her as an indicator of substantial wealth; unlike some of the frequent cruisers she had come to know. Quite the opposite in fact, she thought. Plainly dressed and what she would consider as being slightly 'touched.' "Are you aware that this is a twelve week voyage around South

America aboard the *Athena*—one of the most modern and luxurious ships in the cruise fleet?"

Warner nodded. "Yes. That's the one. Are there still places available?" Ever the pessimist, he clung to the view that, knowing his luck, it would be fully booked. After all, it was only a few weeks to the date of departure.

"I'll just call to find out. If you'll excuse me for a moment." The travel agent got up and went into a back room.

There was no one else in the office and Warner stared for a moment at the phone on her desk, wondering why she had not used that one. After a few minutes she returned, giving him the thumbs up.

"You're in luck. There's one cabin remaining. Cabin D166, which is situated on the port side. Very spacious. Conveniently located mid-ships for easy access. Now if I can just take some details." The travel agent removed a form from a tray and grabbed a pen. "It's company policy that, due to the late reservation, we have to ask for the full payment up front. In this case it will be..." She typed in some figures on a calculator. "Twelve thousand, nine hundred and seventy-eight dollars." It was at this stage, that she thought that her rather peculiar customer was going to start blustering, to make for the door. Instead, he just reached into his pocket and removed his cheque-book.

* * * *

The day of embarkation was one of heightened excitement and nervousness for Warner. Throughout the one and a half-hour coach journey from his home town to the port he had sat fidgeting and fretting over whether or not he had brought everything required; passport, booking confirmation and enough on-board spending money. He had tried to occupy his mind by going through the cruise brochure, truly impressed at all of the ship's statistics; sixteen passenger decks, four restaurants, eleven bars, three swimming pools, an open-air cinema screen, a casino, a playhouse, a fully-fitted gymnasium and a whole plethora of other entertainment venues. In addition to the five star service, he could eat and drink as much as he wanted, twenty-four hours a day, if he so desired. It had a maximum passenger capacity of two and a half thousand, something that truly awed, and if he were honest, frightened him, for since his accident he had become socially impaired, unable to fully engage with others. It had been for this particular reason that Doctor Edwards had suggested this venture in the first place. After all, the ship was in effect a large sea-going village, one in which he would have ample opportunities to meet others. Yes, perhaps it was a bit akin to being thrown in at the deep end, but maybe it was just what he needed.

Upon arrival at the Fort Lauderdale docks, Warner overheard one of his fellow passengers on the coach saying that the cruise ship was now visible. Looking to his right, he saw the luxury liner rising high above the rather grim and unflattering dockyard buildings—a massive, elegant, white floating palace.

Less than ten minutes later, after transiting through the passport control and having shown his ticket, he handed over his luggage and was allocated a red boarding pass. Boarding staff courteously guided him up an escalator towards a large, exquisitely furnished holding area where well over seven hundred other people were gathered.

A slight pang of dread and disorientation struck Warner. Although he had never been diagnosed with agoraphobia, he felt a momentary dizziness. Steadying himself, he tried to put a smile on his face as he looked around for somewhere to sit. There was a bank of empty chairs over to his right. Nervously, he walked over and sat down. No sooner had he done so, than an announcement came over the public address system informing passengers with yellow boarding passes that they should now proceed to the main entrance.

Warner watched as those in question rose to their feet and started to make their way to the exit on the far side. For the next twenty-five minutes he sat in virtual silence, awaiting his turn, self-consciously aware that he had already set himself apart from everyone else. During that time, he surreptitiously observed those around him, realising that it was these people that he would be spending the better part of the next three months alongside.

They were an eclectic, yet obviously wealthy assortment. Most of them were at least a couple of decades older than him. No doubt retired and with plenty of money in the bank and the freedom to now live as they wished. Rich businessmen, some dressed in their suits but most already in their holiday attire and their glamorous wives and girlfriends were also present in large numbers. He could not help but feel somewhat envious of these people whose lives were carefree and devoid of the pains and torments which he had been forced to endure.

He had to shake himself mentally from this growing sentiment of bitterness. This was no way to start his holiday. He should be looking forward to the prospect of a dream getaway instead of sitting here gloomily going over all that he had lost. It was a struggle, but somehow he managed to overcome his sense of resentment just in time for him to hear that it was now time for all of those with a red boarding pass to begin embarkation.

* * * *

Warner was spellbound. Even though he had thoroughly consulted the brochure prior to boarding, trying to familiarise himself with the general layout and the deck plans, he marvelled at the immensity of it. The central atrium—the heart of the passenger part of the ship—was artistically designed and ultra-modern, built over three decks with glass-fronted elevators. Numerous shops and boutiques were arranged around it and everywhere he looked he could see people. Some of them were clearly crew members, outfitted in smart uniforms, broad smiles imprinted on their tanned, welcoming faces.

"Can I help you, sir?"

Warner turned. A young man dressed in a smart black blazer, the logo of the cruise firm emblazoned on his breast pocket, stood before him.

"If I can be of any assistance please let me know."

"Yes…I was wondering if you could direct me to my cabin." Warner shuffled to one side as a fresh influx of passengers streamed in behind him. Most of them seemed to know exactly where they were going, having no doubt cruised on this ship before. Some, however, seemed to be just as confused as he was.

"Certainly. May I have your cabin number."

"D166."

"That'll be on D Deck, mid-ships, on the port side." The young man pointed to the nearest elevator. "That elevator will take you almost straight to it."

"And can you tell me when I will be able to reclaim my luggage?" This was something which had been troubling Warner after having handed his baggage over. He had read of numerous occasions in various magazines of people, mostly travellers at airports, having their luggage misplaced. The last thing he would be needing would be for all of his clothes and personal items not to have been loaded on board. He knew that he would not be fully at rest until he had been reunited with his cases.

"Your luggage will be delivered to your cabin prior to our setting sail. If there are any problems please do not hesitate to get in contact with our reception which is one deck above this one. But please, be assured, all of your belongings will be safely delivered. If there is anything else I can help you with…?"

"No. Thank you." Warner was keen to get away. A crowd had already gathered at the elevator and when it arrived he jostled his way inside. It was cramped, and he was feeling slightly claustrophobic by the time it arrived on his chosen deck. He stepped out, still not fully believing that he was here—and that this would be his home for many days to come.

As he had been told, cabin D166 was only a short distance away from the central landing. It was on a rather narrow passage that ran most of the length of the ship. There were other people out and about, some having already obtained their luggage and who were now in the process of settling in. He paced over to the door, stopping as a sudden announcement rang out, alerting all passengers to the fact that there was going to be a short safety announcement in just over twenty minutes time. It was highly recommended, and indeed part of statutory maritime law, that all should make their way down to their designated muster points in order to participate in a mock evacuation drill which would necessitate the wearing of a life-jacket.

If this message was meant to be reassuring, it had the opposite effect on Warner, whose morbid mind was suddenly made aware of the fact that he would be on a ship at sea and that disaster could strike. Seasickness would be the least of his worries as a myriad of dark thoughts swept through his consciousness.

Apprehension seized him as his troubled thought processes went into overdrive. Were there enough lifeboats to accommodate all on board? Was that not one of the problems that had resulted in so many deaths when the *Titanic* had gone down? Just how effective would a trial run at donning a life-jacket and making one's way calmly to the lifeboats be when faced with the absolute chaos of a sinking ship, the entire vessel canted at an acute angle as it filled up with freezing seawater in the dead of night?

Silently, he cursed himself. Here he was presentimenting worst-case scenarios. Hell, he hadn't even got inside his cabin yet and already he was contemplating disaster. He knew that all of these morbid thoughts were a direct result of his brain damage and his subsequent life experience. To his way of thinking, everything was bleak; shades of black.

Warner gave himself a smack on his head with the heel of his right palm, dismissing, for the time being at least, his negative outlook. Outside his door was a small plastic tray in which was his cabin key and a newsletter highlighting all of the events planned for later on that evening, including dining arrangements. There was going to be a grand sail-away party up on the top decks with complimentary champagne and canapés to which all were invited.

The cabin itself was more spacious than he had anticipated. And, stepping inside, he saw that there was a large double bed, several chests of drawers, a bureau upon which a telephone rested, a sofa, two chairs, and a television. The en suite bathroom and shower was relatively small, but certainly adequate. A large, sliding, floor-to-ceiling glass panel gave access to the balcony.

"Welcome, sir. Let me introduce myself. My name is Pedro, and I will be your steward."

Warner hadn't heard the other enter behind him. He turned to the small, brown-skinned man who stood in the doorway.

"If there is anything you require please let me know." Pedro smiled cheerily. English was clearly not his first language, but he spoke it most fluently.

Warner nodded. "Why, thanks."

"You'll find your life-jacket just under your bed. You'll need to take it with you when you attend the safety demonstration. You'll be in muster station D. Just go right until you get to the next set of elevators. You can't miss it."

* * * *

It had passed midnight when Warner finally retired for the evening, his mind a riot of pleasant swirling images and recent memories. Everything seemed to be going better than he had dared hope. His luggage had appeared, and that was a great relief. The safety exercise had gone without a hitch and, much to his surprise, he had thoroughly enjoyed the celebrations that had taken place up on the top decks, actually finding the confidence to strike up a few conversations with some of the other passengers, of which there were hundreds. He had found everyone so easy-going and friendly that talking had just come naturally.

At the sumptuous evening meal, he had sat at a table with seven others and whilst, initially, he had felt somewhat uncomfortable, he soon found himself, possibly due to the copious amounts of wine that was served, speaking quite freely. And unless he was very much mistaken, there was even an unattached, rather attractive woman who had shown some interest in him. This was certainly the life, he thought, wondering just what the numerous days ahead promised. He had already made some friends and had arranged for a game of deck quoits after breakfast, although he had no idea how the game was played.

As he lay in bed, reflecting on the day, the slight swaying of the ship providing a gentle soporific effect, the realisation that nobody here knew anything about his past was a welcome one to him, for it allowed him to adopt whatever persona he cared to. To these people, he would only be a brain-damaged accident survivor whose life had been effectively ruined if he elected to *tell* them that he was. Providing he didn't have to talk too much, and that his sometimes garbled speech didn't give him away, he could be just as suave and sophisticated as they were. Yes, it was a lie, but so what? Perhaps this would prove to be the means by which he could overcome all that had happened to him. He would like to have known what Doctor Edwards would have thought of this. Given the alternative of wallowing in depression would he not have given him his approval?

Out in the corridor, outside his cabin, he could hear the sounds of late-night revellers returning. He had overheard in one of the elevators that someone was on a winning streak in the casino, something of a rarity on the first night. Maybe they were friends and family of that individual who were celebrating. The noises suddenly ceased and all he could hear was the faint sloshing of the waves.

Blinking the sleep from his eyes, Warner began to stir. Reaching out with his right hand, he felt for his watch, activating the light. It had just gone nine-twenty. The cabin was in darkness, the thick black-out curtains which screened off the balcony doors working exceptionally well. Flicking on a bedside lamp, he was struck with a minute-long bout of disorientation, uncertain as to where he was. And then, with a smile, he remembered everything. He was aboard the *Athena*. The ship would no doubt be somewhere off the Cuban coast by now, heading for the first port of call; Montevideo in Uruguay.

He got out of bed, and opened the curtains, somewhat disappointed that it was foggy outside. At least there was virtually no swell. In fact, coming to think of it, there didn't seem to be any motion at all. Nor could he hear the constant dull throb of the engines that he had been aware of yesterday. Maybe, when there was no urgency for speed, the engines were muffled and power was reduced, he thought.

After he had dressed, Warner finished the last of his unpacking. He had noticed from the overview of the cruise that there were many nights classed as formal during which it was expected for all to dress in their very best. For this reason, he had brought along a hired tuxedo and he was pleased to see that it had not been unduly creased in his suit holder. Once all of his clothes were carefully stowed away, he decided it was high time for breakfast.

After ensuring that he had his cabin key, he prepared to leave. He turned the handle, but the door would not open. He tried it again. Nothing. With a confused grunt, Warner's actions became more forceful. *This was great!* He examined his cabin key, a plastic card that slotted into the door on the outside. There was no corresponding slot on the inside. Futilely, he tried the handle once more.

For a moment he stood there, wondering what to do next. Briefly, he considered hammering on the door until someone arrived, before heading over to the phone. There were several numbers there; main reception desk, room service, emergency. He dialled in the code for the reception desk. The line was dead.

Warner cursed savagely. Things were becoming ridiculous. He paced over to the door and tried the handle again. The door remained locked. He flicked on the lights—at least they worked.

A small germ of panic began to fester deep in his gut. Breathing heavily, he tried to put things in focus. So the door was locked. From what he had read, all the cabins were cleaned and tidied twice every day by the stewards. If he remained patient it would only be a matter of time before Pedro turned up and he could explain everything, tell him all about the door and the faulty phone. With the realisation that there was not much more he could do, he went over and tried to switch the television on. It too, was dead.

Warner gave a dismissive shake of his head. These super-deluxe living spaces were supposed to be state-of-the-art. He had never been one for complaining, but surely this was unacceptable. Of the two thousand or so passengers on board, it would be just his luck to end up in the cabin where nothing worked. Unless…unless there had been something which had affected the entire ship's electronics; such as a pulse from some freakish electro-magnetic environmental occurrence or something similar. The lights worked but perhaps they operated on some kind of auxiliary power system.

For a moment he considered just lying on his bed until the steward turned up then decided he would go out onto his balcony. It was just possible that he would be able to get the attention of his neighbours; alert them to his predicament. Drawing the glass panel aside, he stepped out. It was very foggy preventing him from seeing too much of the ship. On either side was a metal partition which screened off the balcony from those on either side, providing some measure of privacy. Hands on the railing, he craned forward, looking into the balcony on his right. There was no one there and he could see that the curtains were drawn. He went to his left. It was exactly the same.

"Hello! Is there anybody there?"

His cry went unanswered.

Despairingly, Warner returned inside. He sank onto his bed and tried to pull himself out of his current plight by thinking through how he would spend the day. The ship had so much to offer. Maybe he would see what movies were on show or maybe he would chance his luck in the casino. In the early afternoon, in the theatre, a guest speaker was giving a talk on South American wildlife.

No matter how hard he tried to distract his mind, as the minutes dragged slowly on and there was no sign of his steward and, slightly more concerning, no sounds from elsewhere, he began to feel an unwelcome pang of anxiety in the pit of his stomach. Checking his watch, he saw that it was now fast approaching half-past ten. He had surely missed that arranged game of quoits.

With an exasperated sigh, Warner marched over to the door and began hammering on it. His frantic actions got no reply and after a minute, he returned to his bed. Surely someone must have heard him? He was beginning to feel like a prisoner in his own cabin. This was becoming unbearable.

Sitting on the edge of his bed he began to go through the somewhat limited options available to him. Everything seemed to boil down to but one thing—and that was to wait until his steward turned up, hopefully sometime within the next hour. Having reached this conclusion, Warner decided to just lie back and flick through the cruise guide. There remained a considerable amount of deciding which port excursions he would go on and he spent the best part of an hour going through the brochure.

Still no one came.

This had ceased to be a laughing matter. Getting to his feet, Warner stomped over to the door and began to thump heavily on it. A minute passed. And then another. He was becoming infuriated with the whole thing. Angrily, he began shouting and kicking at the door, demanding to be let out. His actions were futile.

There remained one further course of action. Picking up a chair, he carried it out to the balcony, putting it down adjacent to the partition on his right. Using the chair and the railing, he clambered up and over. It was an awkward manoeuvre and he fell with a crash on the other side. Getting to his feet, he knocked loudly on the window. When he got no reply, he went to the far side to see if he could see any signs of activity on the balcony neighbouring this one.

Warner didn't know what to do. His situation had not improved, in fact it had become worse for now he was effectively stuck. Without some means of assisting in the climb over he would have to take a much greater risk by edging out and using the railing. He was now at the stage where he would have welcomed the curtains to suddenly part and the occupant to be stood there stark naked demanding to know his business. Yes, it would be terribly embarrassing and perhaps not the best of introductions but as things were he couldn't care less.

He was pretty sure that he had heard someone in this cabin before he had gone to bed so either they were out or they were still asleep. If he could only get access then he would be able to get out via this cabin. Unfortunately he couldn't get the glass panel to slide across, it being locked from the inside.

Aware that there was little else he could do, he peered around the edge of the other partition and was relived to notice that the balcony door leading to this cabin was slightly ajar. A part of him was now thinking what an idiot he was being and just how much he was over-reacting to what, at the end of the day, was a mundane, rather insignificant problem, for here he was, now risking his very life by climbing over these barriers. One bad slip and he would fall over the edge and plummet sixty feet or so into the sea.

With a curse, he climbed up the side of the barrier using the railing. He then had to get his feet around the outer side, using his hands to grasp onto the metal divide.

Slowly, nervously, he clambered around fearing that at any moment he would lose his footing and be forced to hang on as he desperately sought to regain a purchase. His heart was beating rapidly in his chest as he managed to negotiate the precarious act, pulling himself upright on the other side.

"Hello!" It was practically a scream, a frantic plea for help.

Shaking his head, Warner pushed the sliding window to one side and entered the cabin. It was empty, yet there were signs that it had been recently occupied; suitcases lying to one side, a change of clothes piled on the made bed, personal items and prescription tablets arrayed on the bedside table. The last thing he wanted was for the occupant to return, for he would be viewed with unsurprising suspicion. Hurriedly, he went over to the cabin door praying that it wouldn't be locked.

He turned the handle. The door refused to open. "No! No! No!" Warner began to beat on it, pummelling it with his fists, kicking it with his feet. Why was nobody answering his calls?

For five minutes he kept up his battering until arriving at the realisation that no one was coming. Helplessly, he went and sat on the bed, his head in his hands, trying his best to retain some level of self-composure. This wasn't happening, he tried to tell himself. He looked at his watch. It was now almost midday. People would be sitting down to lunch or congregating in the bars and here he was, stuck, a prisoner in someone else's cabin. He tried the phone but it too was dead.

Time became a strange concept in his mind as he sat there, wracking his brain for a means of escape. Minutes seemed to creep with an almost painful slowness as the frustration and the concern festered inside him. His agitation was now burning like battery acid within his stomach and he looked with some measure of confusion at the small bloody imprints his fingernails had made in the palms of his hands.

A madness threatened to consume him. Rising to his feet he began yelling and pounding at the connecting cabin walls, screaming at the top of his voice to be let out. He was beginning to feel like a caged animal…or a psychopath in a padded cell.

Hefting the television from where it was secured on the wall, he hurled it at the door, making a large dent in it. He lifted it again and was just about to throw it once more when there came a soft click.

Hope leapt into his heart. Dropping the television, he reached out and turned the handle.

The door opened.

Panting heavily with relief, Warner stepped out into the narrow corridor. Seeing no one, he proceeded to the elevators then changed his mind and took the stairs, heading for the atrium and the central reception, a fury building up inside him.

A deathly silence clung to everything. *Where was everybody?* At this time of day he would have expected this place to be a hive of activity, more so when one considered that it was hardly appropriate weather for sunbathing on the top decks.

There was no one at the reception and now real panic began to tear at Warner. Shaking his head with bewilderment, he went into one of the nearby shops, his nerves tingling with fear. Yesterday there had been something in the region of two and a half thousand passengers on board and perhaps half that number of crew and now they had all vanished. It was crazy. Unreal.

"Hello! Is there anybody about?" he cried repeatedly, wandering from empty shop to empty shop. His mind was slipping, unable to grasp a situation that was utterly unfathomable. Deep down a part of him was still trying to maintain a rationale grip on things but as the minutes passed and the scale of his isolation struck home, he began to experience a further slip into insanity.

Supporting himself against a balcony from which he could look down into the area where he had first entered the ship, he felt his mind begin to sag. His legs felt weak. *What had happened?* A numbing sensation clamped tightly on his brain.

Woodenly, he began walking towards one of the dining rooms. Passing a large, gilt-edged, floor-to-ceiling mirror he was shocked at his pallid reflection. Fear and confusion were imprinted on his features.

The dining room was vast, yet empty, its numerous tables neatly set out in preparation for a gourmet, six course meal that in all likelihood would never be eaten. Staggering through the main area, Warner pushed open the doors that led to the galley. Rows and rows of spotless racks containing dishes, cooking utensils, glasses and general kitchenware stretched before him.

"Hello! Can anybody hear me?" he hollered before turning around and re-entering the dining room. He exited by the way he had entered and went to the stairs, reaching the decision that he would continue his search for others on the open decks.

He daren't take the elevators and it was a relatively tiring climb up fourteen flights so that his leg muscles were aching by the time he reached the top. He had only a short walk out onto the open deck. The dense fog obscured vision but he could make out one of the swimming pools and the poolside bar. Countless unattended sun-loungers lay in neat rows. This place should have been packed with people; sun-worshippers and fun-lovers, bikini-clad beauties and leering older men, all living it up by the pool, flirting, laughing and talking whilst they sipped their cocktails and guzzled their beer.

Instead, an unearthly pall of stillness and silence lay over everything. All was shrouded in a thick, grey blanket.

Warner had become sapped by what he was experiencing, both mentally and physically. He felt as though he was in a living nightmare, indeed, as he staggered into the huge buffet area he began to tremble all over. Somehow, he managed to get to a chair and slumped down into it, noticing from a large wall clock that it was now a quarter to one.

He began to ransack his damaged brain for possible explanations.

Could it be that, sometime during the night, there had been an emergency, one that had resulted in everyone, bar him, abandoning ship? It seemed unlikely and he had been fairly sure that he had seen the tenebrous outlines of the lifeboats still in their places when he had climbed over the neighbouring balcony dividers. And surely, if that had been the case, the coastguard would be on the scene by now. Rescue helicopters would be hovering overhead.

Despite the gravity of his situation, or perhaps because of it, he almost burst out laughing as his paranoid mind began to entertain the notion that perhaps he had been drugged and taken from the *Athena* only to have been locked in a cabin on another, empty ship. Something he temporarily called the 'alternate ship' theory. The more he began to think, the more he began to focus on this idea—rationalising that he had been abducted and effectively imprisoned by a nefarious agency, perhaps one that was even now watching and monitoring him, tracking his movements and his behaviour; maintaining a cruel surveillance. Maybe it was all part of a societal experiment or, considering his neurological damage, a psychological one. Yes, that was it. No doubt that bastard Doctor Edwards had set this grand plan into operation. After all, hadn't it been his idea that he should go on this damned voyage in the first place? And why had he been so insistent on this cruise in particular? His thoughts went back to the woman in the travel agency. She was no doubt part of it, the dark conspiracy, arranging things in advance on the phone in the back room, out of earshot.

Warner thumped the table. Jesus Christ, just who did these people think they were?

But then, as his temper began to cool a little, and a modicum of sanity crept back, he realised just how absurd this idea sounded. There was no denying the fact that something very strange had happened but surely this was just a little too far-fetched? It seemed to defy reason to imagine that anyone would go to such extraordinary lengths to create the illusion that he was now aboard a virtually identical yet unpopulated ship. Surely that was pushing the boundaries of believability? Was he not being guilty of inflating his own ego believing he was of such importance?

Everything came back to the same question—*where was everybody*?

Surely they weren't all hiding or hadn't all jumped overboard for both of these circumstances implied that a terrible madness had befallen everyone but him. Was there something unnatural in the fog that engulfed the ship, some strange gas or mind-altering poison that had sickened their minds? Was he immune because his mind was already damaged, admittedly not severely but damaged all the same?

Had they been killed, but if so, why were there no bodies?

A sudden coldness crept through him as a macabre thought came to him. Maybe it was *he* who was dead and he was now experiencing the passing of his soul. After all, numerically, it made more sense that something had happened to one as opposed to something happening to hundreds. He felt his pulse and was somewhat relieved to detect a faint beat. Medically, at least, he was alive. Perhaps it was all a bad dream; an involved nightmare playing out in his troubled subconscious. Maybe he was lying on his bed, dead to the world, with all of this nothing more than a dreadful production generated within his impaired cognition. He had spent months after awakening from his coma, unable to grasp the fact that he had been in an accident. During his darkest hours he had believed that he was in a living hell, yelling his frustration to the padded walls of a make-believe cell.

However, this was different. Of that he was certain.

So what was it?

Alien abduction? A time loop? He didn't think they were in the Bermuda Triangle although they weren't that far away from it either. It was like being aboard a futuristic *Marie Celeste*. What had only yesterday been an ultra-modern liner packed with a vibrant mass of cheerful, fun-loving people was now in effect a ghost ship with him the only doomed survivor, an Ancient Mariner of a sort.

Warner felt suddenly hungry. There was food and drink aplenty, enough to keep him fed for weeks. Madness would consume him far before starvation or thirst would. He rose from his chair and went over to the buffet, made himself several cheese and pickle sandwiches, got a glass of orange juice and returned to his table. It was then that he realised that the clock hadn't changed. Consulting his wristwatch he noticed that the one on the wall was stuck at a quarter to one whilst his now indicated that it was five past one.

For ten minutes he sat there, unable to eat his sandwich, formulating in his mind the notion that perhaps the wall clock had stopped at a quarter to one *in the morning*. If that were so then something had happened during the early hours. Had there been some inexplicable environmental or meteorological event; something that had created a gulf in time and space? As an ex-scientist, he knew the various theories regarding such things but had never given them any real credence.

A fresh wave of unreality crashed against his rapidly disintegrating sanity. For here he was, alone, on a cruise ship somewhere adrift off the Cuban coast. At least that's where he presumed he was. For all he knew he could be anywhere… or any*when*.

A thought came to him. He would make his way to the bridge, going on the assumption that the captain or one of his underlings would possibly still be there and, if not, he hoped to find some evidence pertaining to what had happened. He knew that they kept an up-to-date logbook, detailing everything from current position and chartered course to climatic conditions, so it stood to reason that anything unusual would have been recorded. Finishing his sandwiches, he set off, not fully sure as to what he hoped to find or where he was going, but heading for the front of the ship.

A quarter of an hour later he gave up trying to access the bridge. The security system was such that he would need at least two different clearance keys and without them he knew there would be no way of getting inside. Cursing to himself, Warner headed back to the reception desk.

He got lost on the way back and found himself entering the casino. Banks of electronic slot machines lay dormant. In the centre was a blackjack table and a—

He stopped.

There was a smartly dressed figure—a croupier by the looks of it—standing by the roulette table, idly spinning the wheel, the small white ball rattling through the numbered pockets. His jet black hair was parted to one side and there was an unusual twinkle in his piercing green eyes. He looked up.

"Ah, Mr. Warner. Apologies for keeping you detained for a while but there was a bit of cleaning up I had do before you arrived. Didn't want to give you the wrong impression. Anyway, would you care to place a bet?" His voice was mellow.

"Christ! Am I pleased to see you." Warner walked over, ignoring the other's use of his name and the somewhat unusual, given the circumstances, question. "I was beginning to think I was the only human being on this bloody ship."

The croupier smiled. "I'm not Christ, although I have had dealings with Him over the years. A most annoying fellow if truth be told. And as for you being the only human being on this ship; I'm afraid you still are."

"What? What are you talking about?"

"Well, isn't it obvious? I'm the Devil of course."

And in that instant Warner knew that the other had spoken the truth. It was an indisputable fact. And whereas a normal-thinking individual would have perhaps laughed or backed away, believing they were in the presence of an idiot, he just took a seat at the gambling table. Whether his calmness was due to an influence cast upon him he didn't know.

"Good. Now that introductions are over I'll let you into a little secret. But first, I daresay you'd like a drink." The Devil clicked his fingers and a double Scotch and lemonade appeared before Warner.

Warner raised the glass. "Cheers." He took a much-needed sip, followed by a bigger gulp. There was no fear in his mind whatsoever. Nor was there any inner questioning regarding his own sanity. Had it not been due to the Devil's powers of mental domination he would be a blubbering wreck by now, his mind torn to pieces. Casually, he put his drink down and crossed his arms. "So, would you care to tell me just what's going on?"

"Why certainly. Last night a rather irksome individual began to make some outrageous claims that I took offense to. He was boasting that he was luckier than me, that he could beat me at this and that and so on. I let him win for a time, un-til deciding enough was enough. You should have seen their faces when I showed them mine."

"So you killed him…and everyone else, besides me?" Warner had never felt so relaxed. It was as though he was having a peaceful chat with the best friend he had ever known. A small bowl of nuts had now appeared at his elbow and he helped himself to them, tipping a handful into his mouth.

"Exactly." The Devil smiled. "But being the reasonable being that I am, I decided to spare you. Why you? Well, see-ing as this ingenious invention," He gestured to the roulette wheel, "is one of my favourite devices—indeed it is often referred to as the Devil's Wheel—I made a promise that whichever number turned up was the number I'd save. And guess what?" He set the ball rolling and the wheel spinning.

Warner watched, mesmerised almost, as the white ball clattered along the tilted circular track. There was a tangible inevitability in its final stopping in pocket 'one.'

"And there you are."

"But why me in particular?" asked Warner, casually taking another handful of nuts.

"I liked your choice of cabin," the Devil replied.

"Surely there are others?"

"Yes, indeed there are. But yours is rather unique. Not the cabin itself but the number. You must know that D is the old Roman numeral for five hundred. So your cabin could be read as cabin six hundred and sixty-six. The same number one gets if one adds up all the numbers on the wheel."

"Interesting. Anyway, what happens now?"

"The fog will lift soon and a distress call has already been sent. A flotilla of rescue ships are heading your way. They'll be here in a couple of hours. Once you're taken off this ship you're free to do whatever you want. Count yourself lucky, Mr. Warner. I had hoped for the white ball to end up on zero. But I guess I can't have it all my way. Besides, three thousand, six hundred and seventeen souls is a fair haul for one evening."

"You said you'd chosen to 'save' me. How can you say that, knowing that once the rescue boats arrive and I'm taken off this ship my life will never be the same? It's going to look mighty suspicious when it's discovered that I'm the sole survivor. I'll be forever persecuted, labelled as a Jonah, incapable of going anywhere without being hounded by people demanding answers." Despite his questioning, Warner's tone remained amicable and even. Whether he had been desensitised he didn't know but not once did he think about the hundreds of others that were now no more. Through the windows he could see that the fog was already thinning.

"A valid point, I suppose. I may be many things but I always keep my promises. Now then…just what would constitute me 'saving' you? Let me think."

* * * *

With a fluttering of black feathers the crow seemed to come out of nowhere, heading straight for the windscreen before veering off at the last moment. Tyres screaming in protest, the car skidded to a halt mere inches from the intersection. A second later a massive eighteen-wheel truck thundered straight across its path, going through the red lights, horn blaring, its tyres throwing up a load of spray. The back-draft generated by its passing rocked the car to one side.

"Hell. That was a near one." John Warner was shaking, well aware that that was as close a brush with death as he had ever experienced. He turned to his wife. "Are you okay?"

Beth had been asleep in the passenger seat but she was now awake, her eyes wide and staring. "What happened, John? Is everything all right?"

"Yeah. Just a close call. Bloody driver went straight through the lights." Warner's face was as pale as a sheet, his hands tensed around the steering wheel. "I don't feel like doing any more driving this evening. Maybe it'd be best to head back to that motel we just passed and continue our journey in the morning."

"Sounds a good idea."

"It's strange. But just before that bird flew out I had this really weird image of one of those big cruise ships…"

VISIONS OF A DEAD MAN

Some obsessions can survive death.

Tom Callaway breathed in the faintly musty smell of the old book; a more intoxicating scent to him than the finest wine. There were several empty pages at the front and back as well as some quite decent botanical engravings he could frame up individually and sell on. It was, however, the unused pages that were really of use to him. Carefully examining them, he noted that they were in good condition but not too perfect— just right for his purpose. The paper was verifiably Eighteenth Century and should lend itself to the addition of some nicely judged sketches that would pass as works by some minor artist of the time. In his experience, getting the paper right was more than half the battle in creating a credible fake, and he had a lot of experience to draw from.

In his late twenties, Callaway had come to the realisation that he would make a much better living out of forging artworks than he was able to by selling original works of his own. It had been a bitter realisation at first but after a while he came to enjoy the secret satisfaction of fooling the specialists. He was always careful never to push his luck, knowing that whilst he possessed the skill to forge some of the greats, the intense scrutiny that would be applied to any newly discovered work by the likes of Turner, Raphael, or Monet made it far more likely that his work would be uncovered as a fake. By choosing good but not outstanding artists he made a fair living and avoided coming to the attention of the police. He sometimes felt the lure of creating a new masterpiece. The thought of defeating the best of experts with a truly magnificent work made his heart beat a little faster but always the possibility of being caught had stayed his hand for although they no longer executed forgers in Britain, a lengthy prison sentence was a very real possibility.

Tucking his newly purchased book under one arm, Callaway took the bus home to his north London flat. He had a respectable day job as an insurance valuer specialising in art and had in fact unearthed a few fakes by other forgers in his time. He enjoyed his work, which brought him into the kind of close contact with genuine works of art that one could not obtain in a gallery or museum. It also acted as a useful screen. When selling his fakes, he would sometimes pretend that he was acting for an anonymous seller who preferred to sell a piece rather than pay the insurance premium. It was quite possible that some of the dealers he sold to had their suspicions but they seemed content to keep any doubts to themselves as long as they made money in the long run.

Callaway's studio was his best-kept secret. He had spent a couple of weeks after moving into the top floor flat making an attic room to take advantage of the natural daylight from the two roof-lights. The steps up to the studio were hidden behind packing cases in his bedroom. Climbing the steps, with a glass of whisky in one hand and the book of botanical illustrations in the other, he sat at his work table to look over his purchase. The title: *Notable Flora from the Garden of Abbas* meant nothing to him. He leafed through the pages assessing the quality of the paper and the engravings alike. The prints were unremarkable though pleasant for the most part but he started to get a sensation of *wrongness* from the book. It was a feeling he had noticed from time to time when handling a work that he suspected was a fake. Setting down his glass, he began to examine the book more closely. *What was it? What wasn't ringing true?* The binding seemed perfectly genuine and in keeping with the rest of it. The price had certainly not been inflated and the artwork was the usual fare.

He paused, the only thing about the book that was giving him this weird feeling were the pictures themselves. He had seen a great many botanical engravings over the course of his career and they normally showed an impressive attention to detail but held no clues as to the nature of the artist. Scrutinising them more carefully, he saw that although these were slightly sketchily done, they had a liveliness that stood out. Turning page after page, he could see there was far more of the artist's character in them than he would have expected. He found the artist's name—*Philip Lockier*. Not one he had heard of but he could look him up in the reference books downstairs later.

Picking up his whisky, Callaway took a sip as he considered the blank end pages, trying to imagine various purposes they could be put to. He quite fancied a pair of pencil portraits of a young couple, and perhaps a pen and ink study of men fighting on horseback. That would do to begin with and he would have some pages left for future use. Picking up a soft pencil and a piece of spare paper, he began to rough out his ideas. The act of drawing engaged him totally for a while, as it often did, and it was only the inconvenient absence of whisky in his glass that persuaded him to stop an hour later. As he came downstairs he heard the telephone ring. Glancing at his watch he saw it was nearly five o'clock, still time for a work-related call.

"Hello."

"Tom, Kenneth here. Are you free tomorrow by any chance?"

"Yes, actually," Callaway answered. He had intended to spend the day researching the fine details for his forgeries but guaranteed paid work as a valuer was never to be turned down.

"Jolly good. There's a client in Hatfield who needs to have several works valued, a recent inheritance as I understand it. He's awfully keen to get it done quickly. Could you possibly oblige?"

"Certainly, give me the details," Callaway replied, smiling to himself at Kenneth Musgrove's old-fashioned turn of phrase as he wrote down the name and address. "Right, Kenneth, I've got all that. I'll go there tomorrow and should have the report ready in a few days."

"Knew I could count on you, Tom. I'll telephone Mr. Hodges to expect you." Musgrove rang off.

Callaway pulled out his road atlas and spent a few minutes working out the route of his journey. It wouldn't take too long and he liked getting out of London. Putting the atlas down, he turned to his reference books, searching for any mention of a Philip Lockier. Sure enough, his *Encyclopedia of Artists* did not let him down.

Lockier, Philip. Eighteenth Century English painter, known for portraits and landscapes. Studied in Rome but resided in England for most of his life. Died in 1794 following accusations of sacrilegious behaviour.

A shame they don't say what the behaviour was, Callaway thought with amusement. The entry was very brief and told him almost nothing about Lockier but there were a great many artists like that. Little more than footnotes in art history. He wondered what had prompted him to turn out the botanical engravings. It must have been done pretty close to the end of his life looking at the dates. Perhaps the other work had dried up as the man got older. Ruminating on the changes that failing eyesight and health had brought to various artists, he replaced the encyclopedia back in its customary place and thought no more about Lockier that evening.

* * * *

Turning down the stretch of driveway that led to Rook's End, Callaway was pleased to see a substantial but not palatial house set in a well-kept garden. On one occasion he had been sent to value what the owner had described as 'a few bits and pieces' only to find a Gothic mansion big enough to house a regiment and a mountain of paintings, sculptures and medals. This house looked far more modest.

Mr. Hodges proved to be a genial, slightly frail old man.

"I am very grateful to you, Mr. Callaway, for coming out here at such short notice," Hodges said in a somewhat wavering voice, ushering the other into a pleasant drawing room.

"That's quite all right, sir," Callaway assured him, looking around. "You've some very nice works of art, I see."

"Thank you. I'm very fond of them." Hodges smiled. "I've not yet decided which of my recent acquisitions to keep and which to sell. I'm sure you'll be able to inform my decisions." He directed Callaway to one side of the room where about a dozen pictures were stacked against the wall. "Here they are, and there is a portfolio of unframed drawings as well. I inherited them from a cousin and only took possession last week. As far as I can tell there's nothing spectacular there; no long-lost Da Vinci's or the like, but it's quite a nice collection all the same and I was delighted to receive it." He gestured to a chair over beside a card table. "Will you be all right working in here?"

"It's perfect. Thank you," Callaway replied. "I can give you a rough idea of their worth here and now and I'll make notes on each piece and then write up a full valuation once I've checked on the current state of the art market for them. I imagine it should be done within a week."

"Wonderful! I'll let you get on."

Callaway set to work, listing the paintings in his usual fashion: Watercolour. Twelve inches by eight inches. Maritime scene. Slightly water-stained border. Signed: Henry Dickinson 1825 and so on. He also photographed each one. He was working steadily through them when he came to one that stood out from the rest. So far they had all been rather standard; landscapes, still lifes, two portraits of nobody famous, but this particular painting was a striking scene of lightning in a stormy sky over a churchyard. On the steeple of the church he was surprised to see a crucified figure and it was not a classical Christ but a man in church robes. With the use of a magnifying glass, he looked to the base of the painting and read the signature with a jolt of recognition, *Phillip Lockier.*

The door opened and Hodges came back in, staggering slightly under the weight of a tea tray. "Would you care to join me?" he asked hopefully.

"Thank you, that's most kind," Callaway replied. He hastily took the tray from the old man and set it down. "If you don't mind my asking, how did you come by these paintings? You mentioned a cousin."

"That's correct. They were a bequest from a cousin of mine, Susan Millancourt. We both possessed an interest in art and I was one of the fortunate recipients of her collection." Hodges poured out the tea.

"It's rather an unusual coincidence, but this painting appears to be by an artist I heard of for the first time yesterday— Phillip Lockier. Do you happen to know much about him?"

"Lockier? Only a little I'm afraid. Let's have a look." Hodges bent over the painting, putting on his spectacles. "Yes. It's the one with the crucifixion of the priest, isn't it? I've admired it for many years." Cradling his tea cup in his knobbly-fingered hands, he settled back in his chair. "He was a talented painter who seems to have had a nervous breakdown of some sort in his later years. Developed a fixation with what he believed were the avaricious excesses of the Church. There was some suspicion that he committed suicide after he was denounced by the Bishop of Exeter. Not surprisingly it was probably paintings like this one here that sparked off the trouble. Rumour had it that Lockier was planning to show a series of paintings about the deleterious effects of the Church, the Roman Catholic Church in particular, on those with what he considered as genuine faith."

"That seems a little unwise, especially in an age when religion was so important."

"It certainly was. Lockier was definitely pushing his luck. I don't know if he had a personal axe to grind or if he saw himself as a reformer. Whatever the case, he found it hard to get work at the end of his life and survived mostly on the charity of his friends."

"Was one of them a botanist by any chance?" Callaway asked.

"However can you have guessed that?" Hodges was surprised. "Indeed, Sir Henry Knowles. He commissioned Lockier to illustrate a volume of plants from his own garden. He had an interest in medicinal herbs and the like. It was one of the last major undertakings Lockier completed and I think my cousin, Susan, said that he actually died at Knowles' House."

Callaway grinned. "One thing I love about this line of work is that you find connections everywhere. It just so happens that I bought one of those books yesterday, knowing nothing about the artist and then today I meet you—a mine of information."

"Hardly that!" Hodges demurred. "I would very much like to see that volume some time, if it's possible?"

"Of course. How about I bring it with me when I've completed my report? I usually just send them but it's an easy run out here and I would be interested in your opinion of it." Callaway was glad that he had not taken it to pieces yet. With the right buyer, possibly Hodges himself, he could make quite a good profit selling it on intact and he could always find another book to pillage for paper. The rest of the afternoon passed pleasantly and Callaway left with copious notes about the various artworks and a promise to return the following week.

* * * *

It really was a striking painting, thought Callaway back at home as he examined his photograph of the Lockier owned by Hodges. Putting it alongside the book, he could easily see the similarity in style. Leafing through the pages with renewed interest, he realised that Lockier had treated the plants almost as sitters for portraits. Each of them had what he could only describe as their own character. One in particular stood out. A beautiful rendering of a small, pink flowering plant. The colouring was delicate yet vivid and the engraving had such life to it that he almost thought he could smell the flower.

With a start, Callaway realised that he actually *could* detect a faint, sweet smell coming from the book. He raised it to his nose and breathed in deeply. There was no mistaking it, underneath the musty, old-book smell there was a gently pervasive scent, like a garden after rain. He wondered if it had been used to press flowers in and had somehow retained the scent but it seemed unlikely. He put the book down hurriedly as a wave of nausea hit him. The smell had become stronger, fouler, one of cloying decay. Rising unsteadily to his feet, he made for the nearest window. Flinging it open, he gulped in the fresh air and hung his head on his arms on the sill, inhaling deeply.

"The valerian root can cause a disturbance in the stomach even with the sweeter scent of the petals I added to mask it."

Callaway turned, staring in astonishment around the empty room. "Who's there?" he demanded, wondering for a moment whether he had only imagined the voice.

"A soul in need of help. One who could help you in return."

"What the hell is this?" Callaway cried in a shaky voice. Fear was beginning to invade his body, making his pulse quicken. The tone of the voice was unlike any he had ever heard.

"Don't distress yourself."

A chair moved swiftly across the room and Callaway jumped as unseen hands pushed him into it. "Stop this, whatever you are! Leave me alone!" he exclaimed, fighting hard not to succumb to hysteria.

"The valerian root you inhaled appears to be having little effect on you. It usually helps to calm a person but perhaps the shock is too great. I've been hoping to meet someone like you for more years than I care to remember."

"I must be hallucinating," Callaway gasped. "I don't believe in ghosts. I need to rest." He tried to rise from the chair but as he began to move there was a sigh and he saw a shadowy, indistinct figure appear a few feet away. It was an elderly man in very old-fashioned clothes.

"For the sake of your sanity, I suggest you suspend your disbelief for a few moments." The ghost regarded Callaway with frustration. "I also think a little of this might be beneficial." It picked up the bottle of whisky and held it out.

"From one spirit to another!" Callaway joked weakly but he gingerly took the bottle and took a long pull, then another. *Was he going mad?*

"Very wise," the ghost said approvingly. "Strong drink loosens the mind."

"Any looser and mine will slide out of my ears," Callaway muttered. He was finding it hard to carry on denying the evidence of his senses and either the whisky or the valerian was working, for he felt distinctly less hysterical. He was shocked and confused but didn't feel as if he was in any danger as such. The ghost looked familiar and he suddenly realised why. "You're the figure in that painting of the crucified priest!"

"I am indeed. I was the subject, and the creator of that work. I am Philip Lockier and I have a duty to perform before I may join my God in heaven." It spoke fervently and with longing. "I beg you to help me complete my great work. I've seen that you possess the skill."

"*What!?* You want me to paint you a picture?" Callaway started to laugh at the absurdity of it but a moment later the ghost's hands were on his chest and its face was inches from his own.

"I'm afraid that I must insist. I *will* have your help, with or without your blessing, for my task is more important than the wishes of one man."

Callaway cringed away from the phantom. There was an unmistakable fanaticism in its eyes. "Just…just what do you want me to do?" he stammered.

The ghost stepped back. "I intended to paint a triptych—three works that depicted the ways in which the Church betrays its sacred duty. I only managed to complete one before my death; the painting you have seen—*The Crucifixion of Faith. You* must paint the other two for me, under my guidance. My spirit has been tethered to the book my friend Henry Knowles had me illustrate. He was a loyal supporter and once the authorities had begun to hound me we knew I had little time left. As my health failed he devised a way to continue our duty beyond death and I give thanks for his skill."

"What do you mean?" Callaway asked, wondering if he could make it to the door before the spectre stopped him.

"The book is my tomb, or perhaps my sanctuary. That one copy contains the most precious plants—their essences as well as my illustrations. I put my last strength into it and when my body gave way to death, my soul entered the book." The apparition looked anguished and seemed unable to stand still. "We planned to bring me back a few years later, to continue with our work after that damned bishop had forgotten all about it, but Henry died, thrown by his horse." The ghost of Philip Lockier wrung its hands as it paced back and forth. "He slipped away from the world so fast and I've been waiting ever since." It turned back eagerly to Callaway. "You are to be my salvation. With your hands, your skill, I can finish my task and finally gain entry to Heaven. Some thought me a Satanist, but I will prove my devotion to God, to *God* you understand, not to a self-serving hypocrite in Rome; not to any intermediary. This is the crux of my message, the direct and wonderful communication between God and man that the Church would deny us."

Mad as a hatter! thought Callaway desperately. Dead and insane—not a reassuring combination.

The ghost of Lockier seemed to be making an effort to calm itself down. "If you'll do this service for me; paint the pictures and cause them to be seen by as many people as possible—I will help you in return."

Callaway found himself fighting not to laugh. What could a ghost possibly do for him?

"I can make you the most famous artist of your generation, famed for your own work, not the skill you have in plagiarising others. You have the ability, but you lack the message—to be the best, you have to have a burning need to express yourself; a tale that needs to be told. Help me and I will give you all you need to make your mark on the world."

An image of himself, entering the Royal Academy as a feted artist suddenly swam before Callaway's eyes. He couldn't kid himself, it remained his deepest desire; after all the fakes and the deceptions he still wanted recognition in his own right. From what the ghost said, he wouldn't have to do anything too onerous. Besides, what was the alternative?

As if in answer to his thought the ghost spoke again: "I could force you to help me, drive you insane, possess you totally. I would rather not do this." Its resolve was as hard as iron and Callaway had no doubt that it could do all that it threatened. There really was only one course open to him.

* * * *

On the fourth day after agreeing to help Lockier, Callaway woke up feeling almost as tired as when he had fallen asleep. The ghost was pushing him relentlessly and would frequently take over. The first time it happened was during the stage where Callaway was trying to follow Lockier's instructions as to the composition of the picture; it was to be a giant-like figure bestriding the land and Lockier got impatient with their slow progress. Callaway was horrified to see his own hand suddenly sketching confidently on the canvas without any volition on his part. He nearly ran away at that point but the skill and panache with which Lockier painted had begun to entrance him. For years he had submerged his own artistic style in his attempts to copy others. Lockier was painting from the heart and with passion, and if he was honest, with obsession, and he realised that the ghost had been right; what he had really lacked as an artist was having something worthwhile to communicate.

Callaway had been forced to insist on regular breaks which the ghost had grudgingly agreed to and he tried to draw Lockier out about his life and his art. It was generally unsuccessful and all he could gather was that the dead painter had trained as a priest in Rome for a while before turning to art. When Callaway tried to dig deeper, Lockier would grow restless and announce that if he was rested enough to talk he was rested enough to paint.

Waking up on the morning of that fourth day, Callaway stood looking at the colossus he and Lockier had painted. It was almost finished, so quickly had they worked.

The ghost had not yet greeted him; it usually appeared as soon as he woke up, eager to continue, but today the flat felt blissfully empty. Regarding the work, Callaway couldn't help but admire the vigour of it. He gathered from Lockier that the giant figure was representative of the Catholic Church trampling everything in its path—and that it resembled the despised bishop of Exeter. Whether a modern audience would make that connection he was not sure but Lockier seemed to be certain that his triptych would cause a seismic upheaval in society. Callaway had tried to explain that religion was not such a big deal in the modern world and that people, certainly in Britain, were not so easily shocked. He was finding it hard to comprehend the fervour behind this anti-papal zealotry.

Lockier's reply had been brief. "The abuses of the church will continue as long as it tries to stand between man and God. The very fact that there is still a pope in Rome is reason enough for my work."

Why am I doing this? Callaway wondered. He was definitely afraid of the ghost, the glimpse it had given him of how ruthless it could be left him in no doubt that it could ride roughshod over him. It was more than that however; there was a fascination in this strange collaboration that was almost addictive and he felt his own understanding of art and its power growing daily.

It was a relief however to have a brief respite from Lockier's presence. He found his mind turning to the outside world and he suddenly remembered the work he was supposed to be doing for Hodges. If Lockier intended to exhibit the three paintings together, they would need to borrow *The Crucifixion of Faith*.

The set of notes about Hodges' inherited paintings was still where he had left them on the evening Lockier had appeared and he began to hastily compose his report. It would not be as accurate as he would have liked but Callaway realised he badly wanted a good reason to get out of the flat. Surely Lockier could not object to him taking the report to Hodges and proposing the idea of borrowing his painting for an exhibition. It was all part of Lockier's plan after all. He worked steadily on the report and had finished by the time the ghost appeared.

"To work." It scrutinised the report Callaway had just completed. "What is this?"

"That is the key to our obtaining your first painting," Callaway answered.

"Explain," Lockier said, curiously.

Callaway outlined his plan and waited, trying not to look too eager.

"Very well. I intend to put the final touches to *The Monster of Rome* today. If we complete it you may go. I must have that painting, not yet but in due course. Tell the man whatever you have to. Persuade him."

"May I take your book? I'm certain it would capture his interest."

Lockier glanced over at where the book lay. "I think we will keep it in reserve in case the gentleman proves uninterested.

The book will remain here." The wraith's tone was casual but Callaway was sure he had detected fear.

* * * *

"Can you hear me? *Wake up!*"

Callaway groaned and opened his eyes. The ghostly face of Lockier was close to his and he hurriedly pushed himself back a little and sat up. "What happened? One moment I was putting the final highlights on the figure of the colossus, the next…I don't know."

"I'm not sure. You may've fainted. I have myself experienced this on occasion, after times of extreme exertion. I fear I've been working you too hard," Lockier admitted, peering critically at his face although there was a kind of satisfaction in his gaze as well. "I suggest you travel to see Mr. Hodges this afternoon. Some fresh country air will put you right. I've always thought London to be such an unhealthy place. Too much soot. It's bad for the lungs."

"All right, I could do with a break." Callaway stood up a little unsteadily.

"Believe me, I do understand the strain that our partnership is putting you under and I am grateful to you. Once my work is done, I promise you that it will be worth your efforts. In the meantime, I can only stress how vital it is that we have Mr. Hodges' agreement to loan his painting when the time it right. You have to convince him. Otherwise our work is pointless and I will never be able to help you attain your desires."

"Well, I'll do everything I can," Callaway replied, thinking that as long as he managed to prevent himself from blurting out the truth to Hodges he could flatter the old man enough to persuade him. He had felt a resurgence in his creativity during the days working with Lockier and was eager to have this damned job over so he could start his own work. This accursed collaboration was having an adverse effect on both his mental and his physical wellbeing. His skin had become pale and blotchy and there were dark circles under his eyes.

Gathering up his report, Callaway took one last look at the almost finished picture with a level of satisfaction.

After he left, the ghost of Lockier stood, looking out of the window, watching Callaway's car until it was out of sight.

* * * *

"Good heavens! Have you been ill?" Hodges greeted Callaway with concern.

"A slight cold," Callaway lied, startled by Hodges' obvious shock. As he followed the old man through to the drawing room, he caught sight of himself in the hall. "I do look rather grim I must admit."

"Come and sit down. Now, what have you got for me?" Hodges looked excited.

"Firstly, I'm afraid that I was not able to bring my copy of *Notable Flora from the Garden of Abbas*. A friend of mine has it. He's writing an article about Eighteenth Century outsiders in art and when I mentioned it he begged to be allowed to study it." Callaway had thought up this story on the drive down. "In fact, he's hoping that he may be able to borrow your Lockier for a future exhibition."

"Oh, that would be interesting! In fact I've something that your friend might like." Turning to a side table, Hodges picked up an old shoe box and took out a bundle of letters. "A few days after your visit, I received these from my cousin's executors. They were part of the bequest but had been left out of the original delivery. I didn't know, but she had been in contact with the descendants of Henry Knowles himself, that is how she came to buy the Lockier. She also bought the diary of Gerald Knowles, the son you know." He reached into the box and removed a small, leather-bound book. "It's fascinating! Oh there's a lot at the beginning about the estate; livestock and hunting, that kind of thing. He seems to have been a rather serious, responsible middle-aged man, but then it livens up considerably. Gerald definitely didn't like Lockier and was appalled when his father invited him to stay with them. He was afraid that the artist's unorthodox religious views would reflect badly on the family. According to him, his father was a trusting fool, mad about Lockier and his vision. Here, take a look."

Callaway took the offered book and flicked through a few pages while listening to Hodges.

"There's a good description of my painting as it was taking shape. Lockier had a room set up as a studio where he and Henry would spend hours working and talking. The book of flora was commissioned in 1793 and they worked on it at the same time as *The Crucifixion of Faith* was painted. Then Lockier fell ill. Old age from what I can gather, although he faded faster than you might expect. Gerald writes of his father fretting that 'the great work' would not be finished in time. I get the distinct impression that Gerald was praying for as early a death as possible. He calls Lockier a 'parasite' and a 'viper.' He didn't allow his wife and children to visit the studio and indeed sent them away to a relative for the last weeks of the artist's illness. Well, finally Lockier was bed-bound and the painting still only half-done. Hand me the book, I'll find you the place." Hodges quickly searched the diary and then read aloud: "Mr. Lockier is surely on the brink of death and still he will not let us send for a priest. He claims that he has no need to repent his sins to any man and that God alone can know what is in his heart. My father agrees with this irreligious stance and only worries about the damned picture. He has even talked of trying to finish it himself!" Hodges looked up at Callaway, his eyes bright with mischief. "To my reading, it looks like my painting had more than one hand working on it, which probably decreases the value but this is very interesting!"

"Indeed it is," Callaway replied. The words of Gerald Knowles were hitting him like a steadily pounding rain. To hear of the ghost's last days was bizarre and unsettling.

"Eventually Lockier died and Henry Knowles locked himself in the studio. He didn't even allow the body to be removed but called for any number of plants from his garden to be pushed under the door. After the fourth day of this apparent madness, Gerald and two servants broke the door down. They found Henry sprawled on the floor, barely alive. The painting was complete and Lockier's body was still on the bed where he had died, covered with plants."

"That sounds more than a little strange!" Callaway exclaimed.

"Gerald certainly thought so. He ordered for Lockier's corpse to be taken away and carried his father out of the room. Henry was failing fast and only gained consciousness long enough to make Gerald promise not to destroy the painting. He must have realised that his son wanted to do just that. Gerald felt bound by this death-bed promise and banished the painting to a chest in the cellar. It was only remembered when the latest of the Knowles came to sell the house and most of its contents. My cousin, Susan, had known the family a little and bought a large amount of art from the auction. She later persuaded them to let her buy this diary." Hodges finished his tale, rather flushed and very excited by the drama of the story.

Callaway was having difficulty in keeping calm. "You're sure that Henry Knowles died then, I mean he didn't recover from whatever had befallen him?"

"It's quite clear. Gerald carried his dying father out of the studio and he actually died in his arms."

Callaway frowned—Lockier's ghost had told him that Henry had fallen off his horse. "And it seems that *The Crucifixion of Faith* was completed by Henry Knowles after Lockier's death, in a way that was so good that you would never suspect a second hand had been at work on it."

"I can only assume that Henry was a keen amateur and that maybe the painting was closer to completion than Gerald supposed." Hodges rubbed his hands together happily. "It's all so fascinating, isn't it?"

Callaway suddenly felt sick. He hastily excused himself and fled to the downstairs bathroom. Running cold water over his arms and face he tried to work things out. The ghost had lied to him, that much was certain. Henry Knowles had collapsed and then died while working on the irreligious artwork, not in some riding accident. Lockier's ghost must have taken control of Knowles, just as he had done with himself, and then worked him to death. Staring at his haggard reflection in the mirror above the sink, he thought back to this morning. When he had passed out, the ghost had been worried but also faintly pleased, as if things were proceeding as it expected them to. *Oh God*, Callaway thought, *was Henry's death an accident, or had it been part of Lockier's plan? Had it been some kind of martyrdom or sacrifice?*

Looking at the visible effects that Lockier had had on his health so far, Callaway shuddered. All the promises of becoming a respected artist in his own right seemed ridiculous now and he couldn't believe he had been so foolish. Perhaps Henry Knowles had been a willing participant in all this but Callaway was damned if he was going to die to fulfil the obsessive ambitions of an insane ghost. The question was; how was he going to free himself from its unearthly shackles? He knew it could take over his body, but he hadn't actively tried to resist. Also, how far could it travel? Presumably, he was far enough away at the moment or it would have done something to stop him finding all this out from Hodges. He brightened a little. It did seem that he was safe from it at a distance. Or had it simply not bothered to follow him?

One thing was certain, he couldn't spend the rest of his life in this bathroom! Drying his face, Callaway gathered his wits as best he could. He did have one idea that would at least buy him some time. Returning to the drawing room, he assured Hodges that he was quite all right now. They went through his valuations for the other paintings and then Callaway brought up the *The Crucifixion of Faith* again.

"I really can't put a price on this, especially in the light of the new information you have about the painting's creation. As Lockier was not a particularly well-known artist it would be of limited interest but its value will, I'm sure, be enhanced by the story told in the diary. If you were to think of selling, I would definitely recommend that you sell the two together."

"Oh, I wouldn't dream of selling it. It's by far the most interesting work I've ever owned." Hodges paused. "Although I would consider loaning it for an exhibition as you've suggested. I'd love to see the painting, the botanical book and the diary altogether."

"Wonderful!" Callaway said. "By the way, do you know if Gerald Knowles mentioned the book again after his father's death?" A lot was hanging on the answer but he tried to keep his voice even.

"Yes, he did. Towards the end of the diary, he writes that he gave the book away to the, what was his phrase, oh yes, to 'the dustiest museum' he could find. I think he may've been a little maddened by his father's strange death to be honest. He had promised to keep the painting but he wanted the book to be out of his house."

He may have been the sanest of the lot Callaway thought, and it had confirmed his idea. "I really should be going now. Thank you so much for your hospitality." With promises to stay in touch, he took his leave and drove away. He didn't return to London immediately however but pulled his car into a lay-by to think.

Lockier was either planning for him to die or was quite willing to let him die, in the completion of his masterpiece. Henry Knowles had been in his seventies when he died and it could be that Lockier hoped Callaway—far younger and with a very strong ability to paint—would last long enough for the remaining two pictures. In their sessions together, Lockier normally allowed him to do a certain amount on his own but would take over his body for the more important sections. As Henry had been a botanist, not an artist, Lockier would have needed to be in charge for almost all the time, increasing the strain on Henry's health. Callaway wondered if the parasitic Lockier had tried to find other hosts in the intervening years.

If he had, presumably the attempts had failed. He dismissed the question. He needed to concentrate on saving himself from this death sentence. He could of course simply not return to his flat but that stuck in his throat. He didn't want to flee; he wanted to get rid of Lockier, once and for all. Failure to do so would mean he would forever fear the ghost finding him again.

The innocently titled book—*Notable Flora from the Garden of Abbas*—had begun it all for Callaway and he was hoping that it would end it as well. Lockier had called it his 'tomb, or perhaps sanctuary.' Could it be that the ghost was dependent on the book? Lockier had certainly been reluctant for him to take it to show Hodges. What if he were to destroy it? Would that destroy the ghost as well? It seemed like his best chance, but when would he be able to do it? He knew not when Lockier would appear and had no idea where he went, if indeed he went anywhere at all. It could be watching him even now. If he tried to burn the book, would it not just take control of him and stop him before he could even get a match near it? That was a worrying thought.

He went back over every time when Lockier had possessed him, aware that he had never actually tried to fight against its domination. Yes, Lockier had claimed that he could take control with or without his consent, but was that true? Had the ghost in fact tried this with other people unsuccessfully and so had tried to make a bargain with Callaway?

For a long time he sat there, going over possibilities in his mind until he felt he had a plan that had at least a change of working. With a mixture of fear and grim determination, he began the drive home.

* * * *

"Hello?" Callaway called out as he unlocked the door of his flat and walked into the main room. A moment later the phantom appeared. "You'll be pleased to hear that Mr.

Hodges would be delighted to loan his painting to a planned exhibition."

"That is indeed good. Well done," Lockier replied, looking gratified. He examined Callaway closely. "Do you feel better? I should like to get on with our work if you are able. I have the composition for the final painting settled in my mind."

I've only just walked in the door and he wants to start! I wonder if it's just his obsession or if there is some kind of time limit Callaway thought. It was almost time to put his plan into operation. "I think the change of scene did me good. I don't feel as light-headed and weak." He went into the kitchen and started making a stack of sandwiches with the supplies he had bought. The ghost had subtly discouraged him from eating much and he reckoned it didn't want him to be too strong. Sure enough, Lockier followed him and looked aghast at the plate loaded with beef sandwiches and pork pies.

"I'm not sure that's a good idea. A heavy stomach can depress one's skills."

"I'll be fine. Besides, I've hardly eaten anything for the past few days," Callaway said, pleased to be starting the shift in power between them, certain the spirit had intentionally been keeping him half-starved in order to control him more easily. He took his plate and a bottle of fizzy drink up to the studio and set up the final blank canvas on his easel. Picking up the stick of charcoal that Lockier liked to use for making the drawing, he said: "Right, ready when you are."

As before, he felt Lockier assume control, taking over his body. He paid close attention to what was happening. It wasn't as if he could feel the ghost in his mind. The control was on a lower level, as if Lockier was manipulating the nerves and muscles. Callaway had noticed that although the ghost could move objects around a little on its own it could only do sustained, precise work when it was using his body. He let Lockier get absorbed in the drawing for about half an hour before making his first experiment.

Lockier was only really using Callaway's right hand for the drawing and Callaway slowly tried to twitch a finger on his left hand. It worked, and, moreover, Lockier didn't seem to have noticed. Emboldened by this, Callaway exerted his will power and stretched his hand out to the bottle. He grasped it and brought it towards his lips.

"What in God's name are you doing?" The ghost immediately left his body and was standing beside the easel.

"I'm thirsty, that's all," Callaway said and took a long swig. "Sorry if I startled you."

"I would thank you not to do that again. It's most distracting," Lockier complained, glowering at him. "I need to be able to concentrate. You should know that by now."

Callaway apologised once more and readily relinquished control to Lockier but he felt elated. He *could* break the ghost's hold on him. The next question was whether Lockier ever felt tired himself. Callaway observed Lockier carefully all that day as well as making sure that at the break times he ate and drank generously. It seemed to him that the ghost slowed down in his work as the day wore on and when Lockier declared that they were finished for the day, Callaway said: "We could continue for at least another hour if you want."

"No, no. I must be careful not to exhaust you," Lockier said flatly. "We've done enough for today." With that the ghost vanished.

Callaway sat down, careful not to show just how fatigued he really was. Finishing the last of his sandwiches, he reflected on what he had learned. The ghost was definitely at its weakest at the end of a long session of being in control of his body, but then so was he. The food had definitely helped and the need to free himself of Lockier kept his determination strong. After a few minutes recovering, he picked up *Notable Flora from the Garden of Abbas* and began to leaf through it, his senses strained for any signs that Lockier was aware. He could detect nothing and decided to take it one step further.

Still pretending to examine the illustrations, he wandered downstairs and into the kitchen.

His heart was beating fast as he got a tin of soup out of the cupboard and turned on the gas ring. The blue flame sprang into life. Callaway felt sick with anxiety as he tried to nudge the book closer to the flame without making it look intentional. When the corner of the book seemed to be perilously close, he turned away and started making tea and noted wryly that his hands were shaking. A few seconds later he jumped out of his skin as a terrible roar of rage and fear sounded just behind him. He spun round and saw Lockier hurl the book away from the oven.

Callaway grabbed a dish cloth and raced to the book, holding the cloth to the slightly burnt edge. "Oh my God!" he cried, feigning his worry.

The ghost was terrified and enraged. "How could you be so careless!" It looked truly horrendous; wild hair flying and with blazing eyes. "Idiot! You'd ruin everything!"

Callaway didn't have to pretend to be shocked and scared. "I'm sorry. I didn't think for one moment it would be in danger there. I suppose I must be rather tired after all."

Lockier threw him a furious glance before turning back to examine the book. "You're extremely fortunate it's only slightly damaged. This book is the culmination of my lifelong friendship with Henry, and a tribute to his knowledge and skill with plants. Although we intended to print may copies of it, this was the only one to be made and it is completely irreplaceable."

Callaway was convinced Lockier was trying to explain away his extreme reaction. It was abundantly clear that the book was of supreme importance to the ghost. He had found out what he needed to know.

* * * *

In the small hours of the night, Callaway lay awake. It had been a nervous evening as Lockier had taken to wandering about the flat, occasionally picking up small objects as if distracted, leaving him wondering if the ghost was trying to work out how much it could do on its own. Not very much it seemed. He was thankful for that as he was pretty sure that he would be in immediate danger if Lockier thought he no longer needed an assistant. Luckily, Lockier hadn't guessed that he had damaged the book on purpose. It was regarding Callaway as a clumsy fool, but not a saboteur. That would all change if his plan didn't work quickly enough.

At the end of each painting session, Callaway cleaned the brushes in turpentine as was normal practice. Turpentine was extremely flammable. If he could contrive to get enough properly soaked into the book then it would take very little to burn it to a cinder. Soaked rags had even been known to spontaneously combust. He would have to wait until they had finished the drawing stage and got on to the oils, but that delay might be beneficial. As long as he could keep his energy levels up.

In order to tire out Lockier, Callaway would have to persuade the ghost to do as much of the work as possible. If he pretended to be getting exhausted and made several bad slips it should be easy enough to get the ghost to assume control. On other occasions it had shown great annoyance whenever he got something a little wrong. So it should work. However, it was also possible that the ghost would become suspicious. It could easily turn on him, perhaps it could even kill him and then animate his corpse to complete its ambition.

Turning over all the possible ways his plan could go wrong, Callaway eventually fell into a troubled sleep.

* * * *

The third and final painting of Lockier's great work was also the grandest. Titled *The Infernal City*, it depicted the Vatican as a golden temple to wealth; the poor and the downtrodden living in squalor outside its gilded walls. Callaway had worked well but was exaggerating his tiredness each day resulting in Lockier having to take over more frequently. Out of curiosity, Callaway asked one time what was Lockier's plan for displaying the paintings.

Lockier had paused and asked: "Which is the principle cathedral in England now, Catholic, of course?"

"Westminster, I believe," Callaway answered a little uncertainly.

"Then that is where they must be shown."

"I really don't think they'd allow it!" Callaway almost laughed at the ghost's naive audacity. It would be as inflammatory as putting a portrait of Hitler in a synagogue.

"That is not your concern. You just need to help me create the paintings. Don't worry about what happens after."

I'm not supposed to survive the process, am I? I wonder if you've got some other fool lined up for the next stage Callaway thought bitterly.

* * * *

That afternoon they had a heavy painting session planned and Callaway made sure to foul up almost every time that Lockier trusted him to work on his own. After the fourth mistake, Lockier didn't relinquish control until the sun had gone down.

Callaway struggled to hold on to what little strength he had left and Lockier finally said that they were finished for the day and that he should get some sleep so as not to be so hopeless tomorrow. As he felt the ghost wearily leave his body, he started cleaning the brushes, filling the shallow sink with turpentine. The fumes almost made him faint but he persevered and when the sink was ready, with the brushes steeping in it, he took note of the position of the book on the nearby desk and felt for the lighter in his pocket.

Steeling his nerves, Callaway suddenly grabbed the book and pushed it into the sink, flicked the lighter open with his other hand and thumbed it alight. The effect was instantaneous. The sink whoomphed into flames, setting the book ablaze immediately. However, he had too much turpentine on his apron and hands and these too caught on fire. He started to panic and tried frantically to beat the flames out. He saw the ghost of Lockier appear and shriek with horror at the sight. It reached towards the book but it was already blackening into ash and if Callaway had been able to spare the attention to look, he would have seen Lockier fragmenting into wisps and vanishing with a scream. The rest of the studio was starting to burn now, so much of it was flammable; the paints, the paintings, the papers.

Throwing himself downstairs, Callaway staggered to his bedroom, weeping with the pain. He buried his burning hands in the bedclothes and finally managed to smother the flames but the flat was rapidly filling with smoke. There was nothing for it but to get out. Making for the door, he screamed as a hand clamped on his shoulder and spun him round.

Callaway looked up to see a nightmarish figure which he recognised as the colossus that he and Lockier had painted. Somehow brought to life, it was now superimposed with the insanely shrieking features of the ghost, which was using its last vestiges of strength to take revenge for the betrayal. He was thrown to the floor by the creature, the muscles he had so painstakingly painted pinning him down as the smoke grew thicker and thicker. He could hear Lockier screaming at him but it was becoming muffled as his body began to shut down.

"Vile traitor! Murderer!"

Murderer isn't really true Callaway thought fuzzily, *you were already dead*! Then he realised that the voice was not Lockier's. Another phantom was attacking the colossus. He managed to wriggle free and crawl towards the door.

"I gave my life willingly, but you would've killed this man to achieve your goal. You betrayed our vision!" *That must be Henry Knowles*, thought Callaway weakly. He wondered if he would be able to open the door and get out. His legs were like jelly and his ruined hands were no use turning the handle. *I'm not going to make it* he realised with a kind of fatalism and slumped to the floor, gasping for breath.

"Our vision was more valuable than one man's life." Lockier was protesting but by the sounds of it Henry was not interested. Callaway felt a presence rush over him and there was a mighty crash. The door was open and he gratefully dragged himself through it. Letting himself roll down the stairs, Callaway finally lost consciousness as the entire top floor collapsed in flames.

* * * *

"It's a complete rebuild job I'm afraid. Nothing salvageable in the flat either," the fire investigator said with regret as he visited Callaway in hospital a week later.

"There's absolutely nothing left? Are you sure?" Callaway rasped, his damaged throat still raw, his arms and hands heavily bandaged.

"Sorry, sir. Only ash."

Callaway sank back among his pillows and exhaled. "Thank you," he murmured. Dreadful images tumbled through his head—the terrible conflagration, the shrieking ghost and the awful apparition that had been the painting brought to life. He recognised the irony of it—he finally had something that he needed to paint, to express and somehow expunge from his mind, but his ruined hands no longer had the ability. All he was left with were the visions.

ABOUT THE AUTHOR

As penance for past deeds, Edmund Glasby grew up in Morecambe and studied Egyptian Archaeology at University College London and Archaeology and Anthropology at Oxford—Morecambe, which has more than its share of the strange and unsavoury, provided him with a better education. After turning his back on academia, he now writes in the genres of dark fantasy and supernatural thriller, having been brought up on horror; his father was John S. Glasby the prolific supernatural writer.

2010 saw the publication of his first novel, *Disciple of a Dark God,* a far-ranging dark fantasy epic. His first collection of supernatural stories, *The Dyrsgol Horror and Others* was published by Borgo in 20013, and was followed by *The Ash Murders*, *The Chaos of Chung-Fu*, *Ghouls of the Undercity*, *Labyrinth of the Lost*, and *Dark Shadows*. Currently he is working on two detective novels.

When he is not writing, he is the captain of a local archery club and he has won a trophy or two both at local and European level with the English longbow he made.

www.ingramcontent.com/pod-product-compliance
Lightning Source LLC
Chambersburg PA
CBHW050801250626
47155CB00005B/2160